CW00938632

A Day to Die

It was a twice-told tale along the frontier of California. Willard Flats, a town of gold-hungry, hard-hitting prospectors and power-hungry Southerners who tried to move in and claim everything for themselves, plotting to gain complete control of this rich, new country. The government had been long disturbed by the lawlessness of this new frontier and when they wanted men to break the hold of the wild ones, they chose characters like Rand Kelsey.

The task didn't bother Kelsey especially; he had trained himself to feel no emotion of any kind and he was therefore prepared to kill any man as coldly as he would have killed a rattler if it meant bringing law and order to these frontier towns.

The only question was: could he succeed against all odds?

A Day to Die

Vance Livesey

A Black Horse Western

ROBERT HALE · LONDON

© 1965, 2002 John Glasby
First hardcover edition 2002
Originally published in paperback as
Day of Vengeance by Chuck Adams

ISBN 0 7090 7215 5

Robert Hale Limited
Clerkenwell House
Clerkenwell Green
London EC1R 0HT

Typeset by
Derek Doyle & Associates, Liverpool.
Printed and bound in Great Britain by
Antony Rowe Limited, Wiltshire

ONE

TROUBLE TRAIL

From the top of the hill, the trail ran on for perhaps two miles before it petered out as it hit the edge of the desert. Rand Kelsey eyed it narrowly, watching for any sign of movement, saw nothing, finally wheeled his mount and rode into a thick tangle of catsclaw and vine, the horse thrusting its way forward until it broke free into a small clearing. Swinging down from the saddle, he let his mount go loose. They had travelled most of the day under a blazing hot sun and both horse and rider were plumb tuckered out now that the day was nearing its close and the fiery disc of the sun was sliding down the sky towards the western horizon. It was dark enough in the hollows of the valley to hide anyone who might be watching the trail and maybe they had spotted him earlier, for the dust kicked up by his mount during the long afternoon would have been seen for miles.

The bay remained hipshot near the edge of the clearing and remained like that for a long while. Twisting a smoke, he sat with his back against the trunk of one of the trees, let the sweet smoke trickle through his nostrils. He was a patient man. In the Badlands, time moves slowly and a man learns patience, learns to let the slow march of time take its own course.

He had spotted the dust smudge some hours before.

High on a neighbouring ridge, a few miles back, it had been easy to pick out the pattern of dust which had been the posse from Gunshot, the last outpost along this trail until one crossed the desert that lay directly ahead into California. He had watched as they had swung past him, pushing their mounts in their urgent haste, making a wide sweep through the country and then curving in until they were directly ahead of him, moving off into the distance. He did not doubt that they would ride over the desert in pursuit of him rather than waste any time trying to back-track once they realized they had lost him. The low-down sun now burned like a flame across the ochreous desert, glinting at him through the lower branches of the trees over his head. He was well off the main trail here and shielded by the trees from any other riders who might be in the vicinity.

Tanned to the colour of old leather, his face was a hard, severe mask, hard jawed with thin, closely-pressed lips, the mask of dust and sweat forming white streaks on his cheeks and around his eyes. Even there, there were the deeply etched lines which belong to a man who has looked at a good many things and found most of them to be bad, not to his liking. A quick, sharp, chilly gust swept through the trees and he got to his feet, moving with a rider's loose-ness, eyes half-hidden behind the low drop of the lids.

It would be a cold night, he decided, once the sun went down. Already, it was touching the crests of the tall hills on the far edge of the desert. Just over them, lay the frontier with California. There was dry wood in plenty here among the trees and he lit a fire, heaping the twigs on to it so that it sent out heat but little smoke. Digging into the pack which he had lifted down from the saddle, he brought out some jerked beef and beans, warmed them in the small pan over the flames, boiled water from the tiny stream which flowed through the far side of the clearing and brewed himself some coffee. It wasn't as good as the stuff one bought in the towns, but it was hot and passable. As he ate, he kept part of his mind alert, listening for the faintest sound along the trail in the distance, not expecting anything, but taking no chances.

It was late autumn now, but the richly hued leaves still clung to the branches of the trees around him as though reluctant to leave them. Here, on the very edge of the Badlands, nature seemed to be making up for what lay in store for anyone who continued on the long trail west to the Pacific. The sun dropped with a startling suddenness behind the range of high hills, sent a wave of red, like the aftermath of some titanic explosion rippling over the terrain, filling the hollows with deeper night-shadows. Somewhere in the distance, as if it had been a signal, a coyote howled dismally, the sound rising and falling along a saw-edged scale. The sound shattered the stillness and seemed to beat against his ears, making the coyote sound much nearer than it probably was. The noise ended abruptly on an eerie, rising wail and Rand's face set in a hard line, lips drawing even tighter together.

That's how we both feel, he thought inwardly, *lonesome and curiously friendless*. The years which had passed since the burning tide of the Civil War had swept through the eastern states, had been hard and bitter ones for Rand Kelsey. They had hardened him into the man he was now, with very little warmth and softness in him. Yet something responded deeply to the utter stillness that lay about him. The sombre feeling in him showed outwardly in the set of his face as he rolled another cigarette, lit it and got to his feet slowly, striding to the edge of the clearing where he could part the tall bushes there and look out through the fringe of trees that sheltered him from the view of anyone on the trail.

Coolness flowed against him as the evening wind blew down off the summit of the hills behind the camp he had made. For a moment, he debated whether to ride on through the desert, knowing that in the morning, once the sun came up, not only would he be picked out easily on that vast, flat expanse of alkali dust, but the blistering heat would sap the energy of both himself and his mount.

He toyed with the idea for a long while, standing there, drawing in the smoke from the cigarette, then decided against riding through the night. He had been riding the trail here for close on seven days now, with scarcely a break, except for the previous day which he had spent in Gunshot. He had known there would be trouble the minute he had ridden into the small town. His face matched that on several of the wanted posters plastered around town, another example of the thoroughness with which the Governor worked. He had ridden into that town with a wary eye on the shadows. Knowing that it would have been easy for some bounty hunter to shoot him in the back and claim the reward of a thousand dollars offered for him, dead or alive.

At times, during the long ride, when he had been forced to keep ahead of that posse, he had thought about the man named Weston Clay, the man who had sent him here. They said, in this part of the territory, that when Weston Clay, the Governor, wanted to send in men to break the hold of the wild ones on this new frontier with California, he picked his killers well, men who knew how to handle a gun, men who cared little for human life, who could kill without remorse or feeling, men who had grown bitter and hard over the years. A grim smile played for a moment on Rand's lips. Was he that sort of man? was that how he had appeared to Clay? It had come as a little shock to him when he had first received that message that the Governor wished to see him. When the other had explained what it was he wanted him to do, the feeling of stunned unreality had grown. Certainly he had known that out here, where the big push westward reached its climax, where the red gold which had been found in the hills and rivers of California brought all of the most undesirable elements together, there was a brand of lawlessness which existed no other place in the United States. It needed a certain brand of man to fight such lawlessness; a man as lawless as the killers and crooked gamblers themselves. One was forced to match steel with steel and fire with fire.

Othewise, there could be only one end to it all. A man would ride out with a star pinned on his chest and orders to clean up one of these hell towns; and he would never be seen again, unless one could identify a mound of sun-bleached bones somewhere in the desert as being that man.

The coyote howled again, yapping harshly as if demanding that the moon should rise. He listened to it with only half of his attention. The rest was concentrated in his eyes, letting his gaze run from right to left, from the gentle, green-dark slopes of the valley, out towards the flat, sweeping stretch of the desert to the hills in the far distance, now limmed against the darkening sky, all rises and falls and steep-sided slopes. Almost, he reflected a little sadly, like his own home territory of Wyoming. Back there, of course, the wind would be a trifle colder than here, most of the leaves would have been skimmed off the trees after they had turned into sheets of red and crimson and gold, and the air would hold on its breath just a touch of the winter which was to come.

Dropping the butt of the cigarette on to the ground in front of him, he crushed it out underfoot, rubbing it into the soft earth. The reds and golds in the west had faded completely now. The sky overhead was dark and the first stars were beginning to show. Not a single cloud marred the majestic sweep of the heavens and to the east, there was a pale yellow glow, brightening with every passing minute, where the moon was coming up.

He turned to step back into the brush, then stopped sharply. The sudden crack of the rifle sounded less than half a mile away, down near the bottom of the hill where the trail twisted away towards the edge of the desert. His train of thought snapped off instantly. Behind him, the horse snickered faintly, then was silent. Moving back to where it stood patiently, he pulled the Winchester from its scabbard, pushed the safety off, moved to the outer fringe of trees once more and stood absolutely still peering off into the darkness. He had not heard the approach of any rider, yet that shot had been fired at somebody.

The trail was just visible now, a grey scar that twisted across the darker terrain until it merged with the alkali. As he let his gaze move along it, striving to pick out anything which had no right to be there, he paused, narrowed his eyes, drawing the dark brows tighter together. There was something down there, which he could just make out. A moment later, he was sure. There was a horse standing absolutely motionless close to the side of the trail and a darker shape lying face down on the trail itself. Leaving his mount where it was, he edged swiftly down the slope, feet making no sound in the soft earth and grass. He had no wish to draw the dry-gulcher's fire down on himself, but that man down there might not be dead, merely wounded.

As he slithered through the grass and out-thrusting rocks, he scanned the higher ground for any sign of a tell-tale smudge of rifle smoke, but saw nothing. Probably the killer was using one of the newer Winchesters which did not leave a puff of smoke whenever they were fired as the older Sharp Big Fifties did. Besides, although it had not been possible to estimate exactly where that shot had come from, he felt reasonably certain that it had originated a distance from the trail, over to his right, where the ground lifted slightly to form a long low hump of ground that now stood out darkly against the brighter glow of the alkali. He didn't think that the killer had been using a Spencer either. That rifle would have been far too inaccurate to enable him to pick off a riding man at that distance and to hit a moving target at half a mile, in bad light such as this was, no mean feat for a sharp-shooter.

He dived for a clump of rocks beside the trail, crouched down among them for a long moment, while he cast about him, looking for anything suspicious. He guessed that wherever the killer was, he was likely to come along and check that the man he had dry-gulched was dead. The curiosity of a killer was something which could almost certainly be relied upon, particularly if the other considered that he was alone out here and there was no danger from any other source. Another thing, he reflected. At that distance, in such darkness, it would be impossible for the killer to be absolutely certain of the identity of the man he had killed and Rand reckoned that pretty soon, the other would come along to take a look, just to satisfy himself that his shot had found the right target.

From where he crouched in the shadows, he could just make out the shape of the man lying on his face in the dirt, the horse close by, occasionally nuzzling the body as if trying to make out what had happened to its owner. Rand tightened his lips, wondered if he could risk the quick dash across the stretch of open ground to where the other lay, had his legs twisted up under him, ready to thrust himself forward, when he heard the faint sound. There was a sudden pound of hoofbeats, coming from the opposite direction to that in which he guessed the killer to be hiding. Rand drew his brows together, turned his head quickly, staring off into the dimness. The other could have circled around and come in from the other direction, anticipating trouble.

Then a rider came over the top of the rise in the trail and drove down towards the man. Coming right up to the body, the other reined his mount, paused for a moment, obviously unaware of Rand's presence there, then slid from the saddle and walked cautiously forward. He had pulled a Colt from one holster and was holding it tightly in his fist. Bending, the man felt the other's body, turned the man over on to his back, then got to his feet and stood staring about him, peering in all directions. Curiously, Rand watched him for a moment, then got slowly to his feet, walking forward. The other heard him almost at once, whirled, going down into a slight crouch, swinging the Colt to cover him. Then he froze at once as Rand rasped tightly: 'Hold it, mister. I ain't aiming to kill you.'

For a moment, the other hesitated. Then, reluctantly, he lowered his arm, thrust the Colt back into its holster, held his hands well away from his sides.

'Did you kill him?' he asked thinly.

Rand stepped out on to the trail, then shook his head slowly. 'No. I figured you did. Seems we were both mistaken.'

'Could be,' agreed the other slowly. He still eyed Rand suspiciously, but the Winchester, held on him, stopped any argument he might have had. Rand lowered the gun, walked forward.

'He's been shot in the back with a rifle slug,' said the other, turning a little.

'I know. I saw it happen. Heard the shot from my camp yonder, then picked out the shape of this *hombre*, figured that maybe the killer would decide to come along and take a look-see, make sure he's hit the right man. Easy to be mistaken in this darkness. I was waiting there for him to show up when you happened along.'

Rand straightened up, eyed the other directly. The man held his gaze for a moment, but was the first to look away. He said quietly: 'I'm Jake Danaher. I'm on my way into California. Left Gunshot yesterday and—' He leaned forward a little, seemed to see Rand for the first time and then a look of vague recognition came into his face.

'Say – you're Rand Kelsey!' His voice lifted a little in both volume and pitch. 'You're the gunfighter that posse was chasin'. I saw your picture when I left Gunshot.'

'I never bother to read wanted posters,' Rand said calmly. 'But if you've got any idea of trying to take me in, I wouldn't try it. I don't want to kill you – and I didn't shoot down this man here. You can believe that if you like.'

'Reckon I ain't got no choice, mister,' muttered the other. He stared down at the man lying on the trail. 'Why would anybody want to shoot him in the back like that?'

'Why does anybody shoot a man in the back?' said Rand grimly. 'Could have been some ranny with a grudge against him, whoever he is. This is a hard stretch of country from what I've heard of it, and somebody always has a grudge against somebody else and this seems to be the only way to settle a score like that.' He moved to the side of the trail, climbed over the rumbled rocks there, peered off into the distance where the moon was now rising, flooding the countryside with a pale, cold light. 'I figure the killer must've heard you ridin' up and he's gone now. He wouldn't want to hang around here once he knew somebody else was on the trail. My guess is that he figured there would be nobody ridin' this trail at this time of night.'

'How'd you know he'd ride off?' The other's voice had a higher edge to it now. 'Could be he's still out yonder waiting to pick us off one at a time as soon as we move out into the open.'

'Could be,' Rand agreed. He moved back down to the trail again, glanced down at the prone figure of the dead man. He bent, went through the other's pockets, found nothing that would identify the other, finally straightened up again with a puzzled frown on his face. 'Funny that a man should be ridin' like that without any kind of papers on him,' he said quietly. 'Almost as if he didn't want anybody to know who he was.'

'This ain't exactly the most peaceable territory in the country,' muttered the other. 'Reckon there are plenty of men like him around.'

'I guess so.' Rand drew in a deep breath. 'Well, I reckon that if the killer ain't nowhere around, we'd better bury him. The buzzards will be on him if we leave him around here until morning.'

Danaher laughed harshly. Then he looked away. 'I'd like to oblige,' he said tautly, 'but I've got a lot of distance to cover before morning. I want to cross that stretch of alkali before dawn and, well . . .'

'Then you don't want to help me bury him. Is that it?'

'I'd like to help you, but this is none of my business. I just happened to be along when he was killed. Besides, there's always the chance that the killer might just show up and I'm not handy with a gun and they say you are.'

Rand's lips curled in an expression of distaste. He recognized the symptoms. The man was scared, was look-ing for any excuse that might get him away from that place. Whether he was afraid of a killer who might be hiding out there in the rocks and brush someplace, or whether he was afraid of Rand, and trying not to show it, it was impossible to tell.

Rand stared directly at the other for a long moment, saw the fractional slump of the other's shoulders, then the man turned sharply on his heel, walked back to his horse and swung himself up into the saddle. The dark face and eyes showed one quick flash of triumph, then he had pulled hard on the bridle, taking the horse past Rand and the body. Touching spurs to his mount's flanks, Danaher rode swiftly along the trail, turned a bend in it some three hundred yards away and was gone from sight although the hard tattoo of his mount's hooves on the hard, sun-baked dirt continued to be audible for several minutes, fading swiftly into the distance.

Rand shrugged, laid the Winchester on the ground nearby and moved a few feet off the trail to where the ground was sufficiently soft for him to scoop a hole in which to bury the man. He felt an odd metallic taste at the roof of his mouth as he dug methodically, using his hands and a piece of wood he had found lying close by. The stillness reached in and clammed around him. Death was a hell of a thing, he pondered as he dug. Although he had seen it many times during the past few years, he had never really grown used to it. He did not even know who this man was, his name, nor where he came from, nor even where he had been going when the bullet had taken him in the back, pitching him forward out of his saddle, sending him into the blackness of the long sleep. A good man, or a bad one? There was no way for him to know. It seemed a hell of a way to finish, out here in the wilderness where it swept down to the Badlands. An unmarked grave just off the trail, buried deep enough so that the coyotes would not find you.

He dug with these thoughts moving around in his mind, kept on digging until the hole was up to his waist and decided that would be deep enough, especially if he covered it in with some of the heavier, larger stones from the side of the trail. Pulling himself out of the hole, he stood for a moment, rubbing the muscle of his arm, drawing back his shoulders. The man's horse still stood in the shadows of the rocks, patient, not understanding. It watched as he lifted the lifeless body, carried it to the open grave and lowered it down. Once that was done, he wasted no time shovelling the dirt back in, finishing it off with some of the boulders, packed tight and high over the fresh-turned earth.

Satisfied, he moved towards the horse. While still ten feet from the animal, it suddenly came to life, lunged forward, hooves hammering on the dusty trail, racing into the moonlight until it was gone. Rand shrugged, moved slowly up the slope until he was back among the trees. The fire was still burning where he had left it and he hunkered down beside it, staring into the leaping flames. How he knew that the dry-gulcher was no longer in the vicinity was something he did not pause to question. There were times when a man was sure of something without knowing the reason why. The appearance of Danaher would have scared him off unless he was the sort of man who got a kick out of killing folk from cover, when he might have hung around on the chance that he could have dropped the other without risking his own life.

Placing more, thicker, branches on the fire, he pulled his blanket from the roll, unloosened the cinch around the horse's belly and let the saddle drop to the ground where he lifted it and placed it carefully near the fire as his headrest. Stretching himself out, he lay on his back, feeling some of the warmth from the leaping flames soaking into him, watching the dark cloth of the sky over his head and the stars that hung with a bright glittering in it, so close that he had the unshakeable feeling he had only to lift his hand to be able to touch them, to pull them down to him out of the heavens.

He thought for a while of the man he had buried out there beside the trail, wondered briefly who he might have been and why that killer had been lying in wait for him out there among the rocks, shooting him in the back without any warning. Or had the killer known who he had been shooting at? There was always the chance that he had made a mistake, that he had been watching for someone else and had fired at the first rider to come along that particular stretch of the trail. Maybe the killer had been lying in wait for him. He twisted his lips into a scowl as the thought went through his mind. It seemed likely. After all, he had given that posse the slip and if anyone was waiting for him along this part of the trail, they would have known that, would have been waiting for him to come along. Hell of a thing, he thought idly, when you never knew whose hand might be turned against you, nor who your enemies were.

Acting on impulse, he withdrew one of the Colts from its holster, checked the chambers, then placed it under the blanket where he could reach it at a moment's notice. The flames crackled around the dry twigs and branches and in the soft haze of warmth from the fire, he fell asleep.

The morning was half gone and the heat head was surging swiftly to the peak of its piled-up intensity. Nothing relieved it. Out here in the desert, with the white, burnt alkali dust all about him, with a mask of it on his face where it had mingled with the sweat that streaked his cheeks and forehead, the glare of the sun was a terrible, deadly thing. The glaring disc burned like a furnace in the cloudless heavens and the metal pieces of his bridle sent hard, painful flashes into his eyes as he rode, head bowed a little over the saddle horn.

There was no kicked up dust in the air, except that lifted by his own mount and he knew that there had been no riders headed along this stretch of trail for some time, possibly not since Danaher had ridden out the previous evening. He reversed and lifted his neckpiece over the lower half of his face. His body tightened as he sat easily in the saddle, well forward, to ease the burden on his mount.

When a man had long distances to cover, he rode slowly and easily, letting his mount pick its own gait.

The alkali dust was fine and in places, his horse slipped into it almost up to its fetlocks. He kept wanting to stop, but Rand pushed him on. They had a long way to go before they reached the far edge of the desert and the worst of the day was yet to come. He had allowed the horse a little to drink before they had set off at first light. It had not been as much as the animal had wanted, nor as much as he had wanted when he had drunk some at the stream in the small clearing on top of the hill, but it was always better to make a dry ride than to sweat out pints of water.

The first water hole they came to was nothing more than a scooped out hollow in the whitish dust, the earth baked a little harder than elsewhere, cracked here and there where the last of the water had dried out, evaporating in the hot sun. But already, the dust was sifting in at the edges, smoothing off the hole. Soon, if there was no rain, the water hole would vanish altogether and there would be nothing to indicate where it had been.

Lifting himself a little in the saddle, he shaded his eyes against the wicked, vicious glare of the sunlight. The desert seemed to stretch ahead of him as far as the eye could see and the tall hills on the far side were as far away from him as they had been when he had started out that morning, more than five hours earlier. Shaking his head a little, he screwed up his eyes and tried to pick out any landmark there, but as far as he could see, in every direction, the desert was flat and featureless. Heat was a heavy, burning pressure on his back and shoulders and all about him, where it touched the desert itself, it was thrown back at him, filled with the bitter smell of the alkali and dried-up grass, baked by the strong sun.

Man and rider moved steadily and slowly over that tremendous expanse of burned dust. Rand wanted to dig spurs into the horse's flanks, make it run so that they could be out of this terrible place as quickly as possible, but he fought down the urge with a conscious effort, rubbed some of the sweat out of his eyes. This was one of those stretches of country which could never be tamed, no matter how hard one tried. A gigantic dust bowl that sucked all of the sunlight from the sky, sent all of its moisture back, a dried-out charnel place where nothing grew except for a few scattered clumps of mesquite and cactus and the dried-up roots of bitter grass which somehow managed to suck what little water they needed from the dry dust.

High noon found him riding a deep, wide, steep-sided gully, a natural cleft in the ground, some thirty feet below the level of the desert. The trail itself ran through this spot for men had found that here lay the only bit of shade in the whole stretch of desert. Even at high noon, the walls of the cleft were sufficiently steep and high to provide a little shadow from the blazing sunlight and although the air was hot, possessing an inferno heat as if it had just been drawn through a gigantic oven at red-heat, there was no longer the vicious glare that hurt the eyes and sent stabs of pain through the skull. He rode slowly now, leaning forward a little in the saddle, feeling the dull weariness lie heavily on him. The breeze picked up tiny flurries of dust and threw it down into the gully, covering his face and hand with a thin film of itching grains, working its way inside his clothes so that his entire body seemed on fire with the itching irritation.

Every breath he drew into his lungs was an aching, burning, torturous thing, firing his chest, giving little refreshment to him. Thirty yards further on, the floor of the gully began to lift, would bring him back into the streaming sunlight, back into that terrible, eye-searing glare. Reluctantly, he edged the horse forward. There was a sudden movement at the corner of his eye, a darting shape that skipped from one flat-topped rock to another. He jerked his head around. The sand lizard stared down at him with unwinking eyes as if looking upon him as some other kind of strange animal, representing no danger. It made no further movement as he came level with it, then rode past.

Sunlight struck him like a physical thing, sent pain jarring redly through his eyes even though he screwed them up tightly in an effort to shut most of it out. Glancing ahead, he reckoned that he might have crossed most of the desert by moonrise, then he would head into the low foothills before making camp.

A mile further on, he came across another water hole. He had not expected to find water anywhere in this vast desolation, felt a momentary surprise as he saw the sun glitter off the sluggish, muddy water that stood in the hole. Less than six inches deep, it looked dark and bitter. But his mount drank from it and he knew it wasn't poisoned. Drinking from his canteen, he quenched his thirst, then filled the water bottle from the pool, corking it and slipping it back into its pouch on the saddle. At least he would not go thirsty before he got to the other side of the Badlands.

He let the horse have time to blow, rolling himself a cigarette, lighting it and dragging the sweet-smelling smoke down into his lungs, enjoying it now that his throat was no longer quite so raw and parched. There was a low rise fifty yards from the water hole and moving towards it, he climbed the treacherous, slippery slope, stood on top, peering in every direction. There was nothing to indicate that he was being followed and from his vantage point it was possible to see almost to the very limits of the desert. Only the faint, shimmering haze of his own dust track hung in the air, settling slowly. He waited there until the blazing disc of the sun slipped past its zenith and began its downward slide to the western horizon. The heat was still as heavy, still made the same punishing demands on both man and horse, but it would be getting cooler soon and he knew that the worst of the heat would soon be past.

Gradually, the hill in the distance approached as the long afternoon dragged out its seemingly interminable course. Not once did he look back as he crossed the last stretch of the desert. He thought he made out the shape of a ranch house nestling among the foothills just beyond where the desert petered out, but the glaring sunlight was shining directly in his eyes now so that he could not shade them against it, and it was difficult to be sure of what he saw. He rode across the bottom of a long, dried-out creek, breathed down dust into his lungs, thoughts drawn inward into the steady silence that dwelt within him. These thoughts were what had shaped and tempered him since the fiery holocaust of the Civil War which had changed his entire life. They had made him what he was now; hard and cold and bitter, a lonely man who rode a long and lonely trail. A long, snaking river flowed sluggishly across the trail at the very edge of the desert. He forded it with ease, stopped on the opposite bank, rested up for a little while, strangely content now that the worst was past. Here, there was a welcome touch of greenness on which he could feast his eyes and the tall hills, marking the frontier at this point blotted out the direct rays of the setting sun, sent a wave of coolness down into the valley and the lower slopes that was like a balm on his scorched features. He bent, washed the dust from his face, felt the mask crack as the water touched it, burning his skin underneath. It had been that hot and yet he had scarcely realized it could have burned him like that. Lying flat on his belly, he drank the cool water until he had had his fill, until he could swallow no more, then stretched himself out on his side, rolled a smoke and surrendered himself for a while to the utter weariness that was in his limbs. He felt taut and brittle, like a plank which had lain in the hot sunlight for too long until it had become hard and warped.

The last rays of the setting sun touched the peaks of the hills that lay all the way along the western horizon, touched them with a brilliant flash of flame. It lingered there for a brief while and then dimmed swiftly. The sky over the hills darkened slowly.

Wearily, he got to his feet, stretched himself, tightened the buckle of the gunbelt around his middle and went over to the horse, standing patiently by the bank of the river. Swinging up into the saddle, he sat for a moment looking about him, eyes narrowed a little, taking in every detail of his surroundings. There was the chance that the posse which had lost his trail the previous evening might have decided to wait up here for him crossing the desert. From these hills they would have every chance of spotting a man crossing the flat, rolling expanse of the Badlands.

Riding slowly away from the river, he let his gaze wander slowly from side to side of the trail. The timberline started halfway up the slope and he eyed it apprehensively. If there was anyone lying in wait for him, that was undoubtedly where they were likely to be, the one place where they could wait for him to get within range of their guns without exposing themselves to his return fire.

His horse's feet dropped scarcely a sound on the soft, moist earth and except for the faint, metallic jingle of the metal parts on the bridle, there was no sound about him.

A few moment later, before he reached the foot of the hills, he smelled smoke, drifting on the slight breeze. It was undoubtedly wood smoke, but not that which came from some camp fire. Turning his mount, he touched rowels to it, felt it respond. There was, he reflected. something definitely sinister about the smell of smoke here. Why it should trouble him this way, he wasn't sure; not until he rounded a bend in the trail, breasted a low rise, and found himself looking down on a smooth stretch of grassland, fenced around with a gate swinging loosely on shattered hinges. Beyond the fence, lay the still-smouldering remains of a ranch house. He reckoned it could have been the one he had spotted from the desert, although then, he had been fairly sure he had seen no smoke.

The burning uprights and the resinous flame which still licked around them stilled him and he sat for several moments staring down at the scene of destruction before moving slowly towards it, through the smashed and broken gate which swung creaking in the wind, and over the soft grass which fronted the house. Whoever had done this job had made a thorough burning of it, he thought fiercely. The sharply acrid stench of the smoke stung at the back of his nostrils, and his keen eyes took in the way everything had been burned, the furniture so badly ravaged by the flames that most of it was barely recognizable. He studied the small barn which had once stood beside the house. Now it was a smouldering shell, the roof fallen in, smoke still hanging in a screen over it.

Slipping from the saddle, he walked forward to examine the debris more closely. The wind, keening down from the higher points of the hills covered all other sound except for the rusty shrieking of a windmill wheel which still turned in spite of all that had happened here. At the low porch, he hesitated, then pulled a Colt from its holster, held it in a tight grip as he edged forward, passing in through the low doorway. His blood was hammering in his veins as he moved inside the burned building, not knowing what he was going to find here. This territory was reputedly clear of warlike Indian tribes. The few who were here were supposed to be at peace with the white settlers and he had heard nothing of any warlike acts against the white men. There was a certain grimness in his mind as he cast about him in the dimness, straining his eyes to pick out the details of the room which faced him. There were always Indians who would turn and become renegades, going on to the warpath at the slightest excuse. Tensed, he peered about him. The stench of smoke was strong in his nostrils, and it was blended with other indefinable odours which he did not like nor did he recognize.

Slowly, he moved through the fire-ravaged interior of the house, going from one room to another, checking them all in turn. In the bedroom, he found the bodies of a man and woman. They were lying on the floor in one corner of the room and he bent, wrinkling his nostrils a little, as he turned them both over. When he straightened up, he knew for certain that it had not been Indians who had done this as he had first suspected. Both had been shot in the back.

He went back outside, moving with cat-like silence now. There was just the chance that whoever had done this, was still around. Certainly the attack which had wiped out this couple and their home, had taken place only a short while before.

In the darkness, nothing moved. He stayed within the shelter of a clump of hickory while he listened to all of the faint night sounds. There was nothing there to give him caution. For a moment, he turned and surveyed the scene of destruction behind him, then moved towards his mount. He grew anxious to be away from this place, to make camp somewhere up in the hills, somewhere off the trail and away from the usual routes which men took.

Swinging into the saddle, he stayed with the main upgrade trail for perhaps half an hour, then pulled suddenly off it, into the trees. There was scarcely any undergrowth here and he was able to make good progress. The timber which closed around him was evidently first-growth pine, tall and slender, with no branches to mar the trunks until more than thirty feet from the ground where they then spread out to form an almost impenetrable cover overhead, shutting out the sky and the first stars. Considering the direction in which he guessed the killers had gone, he set his course accordingly, moving upgrade all of the time, keeping roughly parallel to the main trail through the foothills. Here, he reckoned the country would be more broken and afford him with plenty of cover if necessary.

This country was new to him but he felt no concern. He was used to riding these fresh and lonely trails. The war had done this to him. Had there been no fighting, he would probably have been well content to settle down as his brothers had done in Wyoming. But the war had done things to him, as it had to many of the men who had fought through those long campaigns, had hardened him, filled him with a restlessness which nothing could still. Since those days, his life had been a pattern of hills and plains, desertlands and great rivers, high-noon heat and

midnight cold. His home had been somewhere under the
stars, lying in his blankets on the rim of light thrown by his
camp fire. He had long since lost any need of human
companionship.

He came out into the open, where the trees fell away
and there was an area of tumbled rocks and boulders
before him, fluted and etched into fantastic shapes by
long geological ages of wind and rain. Far off, in the
distance, there came a solitary starved echo, a faint mutter
of sound which was not repeated although he listened
intently for it, trying to ascertain what it had been. Riding
on, allowing his mount to pick its way through the boulders, he came presently on an old Indian trail, swung on
to it. Once, long ago, red men had used this trail during
their endless migrations. Now it lay deserted in the faint
yellow moonlight which slanted along the slope of the
hills.

He rode until the white moon had lifted clear into the
heavens, then swung off the trail where it reached a level
stretch of ground. In front of him, the narrow track ran
into rougher ground, sharp-backed ridges and narrow
canyons. There was a shallow creek a few yards off the trail
and he made camp beside it, building his fire in the shelter of a clump of trees, drew his blankets a short distance
beyond the ring of firelight and settled down for the
night, listening to the murmur of the wind in the tree
branches, a chilly wind at this elevation, rustling through
the leaves. Overhead, the darkness was complete now, with
the sharp glitter of a thousand stars standing out in the
black velvet of the night, the moon dimming the stars
close to its own radiance, painting a pattern of light and
shadow along the nearby trail. He lit a cigarette as he lay
there in his blankets, felt the contented ease of the close
of the long day come upon him, relaxing him a little.

TWO

WARNING

It was well after midnight when Kelsey woke, sometime during that period of utter stillness when the whole world seemed asleep, totally alien to sound, yet with that curious waiting quality as if it were breathing quietly to itself, still watchful and alert. He lay quite still for a moment, listening tautly, waiting for the sound which had penetrated that part of his mind which never slept, to repeat itself. Then he heard it again, somewhere far off along the trail. The pounding of a running horse, coming on fast and yet unsteadily, as if it were being ridden by a man either too tired or too badly hurt to worry about where he was going, or the chances he was taking, riding at that speed along a bad trail in the moonlight.

Sliding from under the blanket, he eased himself to his feet, moved out close to the edge of the trail after kicking out the last traces of the glowing fire. The horse came on and he suddenly realized that it was on the narrow trail and not the main trail further down the slope of the hill. Gently, he eased one of the Colts from his belt, steadied it in his hand and crouched down, waiting.

From below him, he heard the crash of iron-shod hooves on hard granite and three minutes later, picked out the lone rider as the man climbed the steep part of the trail. For a moment, it seemed as though the horse would slip on the treacherous rocks and plunge over the edge of the trail, taking its rider with it in that last, long drop on to the main trail below, but it managed to keep its balance, struggling upward until it hit the level stretch and come forward among the rocks and boulders. In places, giant boulders almost filled the trail and the horse was forced to slow as it approached the spot where Kelsey crouched hidden.

The rider drifted in out of the moon-thrown shadows. Kelsey had time to see that he rode slumped forward in the saddle, head bowed on to his chest. Then he stepped out from behind the rock, Colt levelled on the other's chest.

'Hold it right there, mister!' he said sharply.

The horse reared up at the sudden sound, slithered to a halt. As it did so the man released his hold on the reins, made an attempt to hold himself upright, then fell sideways out of the saddle, hitting the ground with a sickening thud. Holstering the gun, Kelsey ran forward, went down on one knee beside the other, his hand feeling for any wound on the man's body. He found none such as he had been looking for. Then he moved sideways a little, so that the flooding yellow moonlight fell full on the other's face and a sharp exhalation left him as he saw the marks on the man's face and neck, the tattered clothing he wore. Gently, he ran his fingers over the other's flesh just beneath the jaw bone. He did not have to think twice as to the cause of those marks. He had seen them on several occasions in the past when men had been strung up from the nearest convenient tree after a lynching party had caught up with them.

This man had been strung up and left to die, but somehow, God alone knew how, he was still alive, had cheated death at its own game. The mark of the rope was plainly visible on his neck and there were deep scratches on his face, one cheek drawn up by a freshly-made scar, cut deep into the flesh so that it pulled his upper lip up at one corner, giving him an oddly leering appearance.

He was barely conscious, lying there, with the air rasping in and out of his chest. Bending again, Kelsey picked up the limp form, surprised at the lightness of it, and carried the man to the fire, laying him down on the moss. Going over to the creek, he fetched back a hatful of cold water, splashing it on the other's face. The man opened his eyes, coughing and spluttering. He tried to push himself to his feet, but Kelsey thrust him back, gently but firmly.

'Lie still while I take a look at you, stranger,' he said harshly. 'Looks to me as though you've been in trouble.'
The other resisted for a moment, then lay back with a faint sigh. His voice was a faint whisper. 'You don't look like one of Sutton's men.'

Kelsey shook his head slowly. 'I never heard that name before,' he said honestly. 'Was he the one who did this?'

'That's right. Name is Meston. Was riding scout for old man Thorpe when he brung one of the wagon trains out here from back east. We crossed the border a couple of weeks ago, headed straight for Willard Flats. That's a town just across the border. We aimed to stay there for a while, get more supplies and then move on to where there's land for the taking, gold if you want to dig for it.'

'But you didn't make it,' Kelsey said. He hunkered back on his heels, waited for the other to go on. This was the kind of story he had heard about, even a hundred miles east of here. The border towns were nearly all in the hands of ruthless killers, crooked gamblers, power-hungry men who stopped at nothing to gain their own evil ends.

Meston swallowed, lifted his right hand and rubbed the a scar on his cheek. He winced as his fingers touched the raw, ragged flesh. 'They claimed there was a tax on every wagon goin' through the town, using that part of the trail. 'They also said we had to pay ten dollars a head for every man, woman and child with the train. Claimed it was the law of the territory.'

'I never heard of any such law,' Kelsey said grimly.

'Neither did we. But they had a marshal there with a

badge on his shirt and he warned us there'd be trouble if we didn't pay up. Old man Thorpe said he'd be damned if he'd be blackmailed by any crooks, that he'd drive the train clear through the town and he'd personally shoot any man who tried to stop him. They let us get to the other side of Willard Flats, and then jumped us. Killed seventeen and took the rest back into town. They strung six of us up, said it would make an example for anybody else who was fool enough to try to drive through without payin'. Reckon that only a frayed rope kept me alive. They hung old man Thorpe. He was dead when I got to him after dark. Managed to steal myself a horse and headed back out of town. Don't recall much of what happened once I left the main trail yonder. Just remember figurin' that I'd better stay off the trail in case they should come after me.'

Kelsey sat back just inside the ring of moonlight at the edge of the clearing. 'You were plumb lucky,' he grated. 'I came across a homestead that had been fired a while back and the two folk inside had been murdered, shot in the back. Whoever did it couldn't have been far along the trail ahead of me when I holed up here for the night. They must've just missed you.'

Going back to the fire, he knelt, blew on the faint glow still present in the heart of it until the red sparks caught on the fresh, dry timber he had heaped on it. Meston lay a few feet away, watched him out of the corner of his eye, his gaze frankly curious and speculative. Finally, he stirred himself a little as Kelsey placed the can of coffee over the flames to heat.

'You must be new to these parts, mister,' he said at last. 'You on the run from some trouble?'

'No.' Kelsey shook his head slowly. 'Just ridin' west. Heard tell there was land to be had in California – good land. Gold, too, if you were lucky.'

Meston sighed. 'That seems to be the reason why they all come here,' he murmured. There was a faint trace of sardonic humour in his tone. 'Lookin' for gold. If they only knew what lay ahead of 'em, mebbe they'd never come.'

'Such as?'

The other coughed hoarsely, seemed to have trouble getting his breath, rubbed his neck gingerly with his fingers. 'Most of 'em spend years in the hills west of Willard Flats, panning the streams, digging in the rocks, without finding a trace of dust. Some make a lucky strike, only to get it all taken from them in the saloons. When they've lost the lot, they head back to the strike. Reckon if they're lucky they ain't followed. More often than not, Sutton sends a couple of his boys after them.'

Kelsey gave a quick nod of understanding. Pouring the coffee into a couple of tin cups, he handed one to Meston, sipped the other himself. Checking his stores, he brought out some jerked beef, placed it in front of the other and sat back on his haunches as the other ate ravenously. He did not speak until the plate was clean.

'Been hidin' out in the hills all day,' he explained, wiping his mouth with the back of his hand. 'Tried to shoot me a deer during the afternoon, but it got clean away.'

'You figurin' on ridin' back east?' Kesley asked. He rolled himself a smoke, offered paper and tobacco to the other.

'Ain't carin' much where I ride, so long as I get away from this stretch of territory.' The other sucked the smoke gratefully into his lungs, stared up at the dark velvet of the heavens overhead.

'There's desert in that direction,' Kelsey told him slowly. 'I've just crossed it. Only one waterhole the whole way. You reckon you feel up to that kind of travel?'

'You got any other suggestions?' asked the other wearily. He sank back on to the ground weakly as if the talking had wearied him. 'If you got any sense, you'll ride back the same way you came.'

'Guess I'm one of those hombres who's always on the look out for trouble.'

Meston let his glance fall to the twin Colts at the other's waist, gave a slow, appraising nod, eyes glittering brightly in the firelight. 'You sure look like a man who can handle a gun,' he agreed finally, 'but what can one man do against a bunch of killers like that, no matter how gun-fast he is?'

Kelsey pursed his lips into a thin, tight line. 'From what you say, I reckon it's about time that somebody made a try.' He drew the last smoke from his cigarette, then flicked the glowing butt into the heart of the fire. 'You'd better get yourself some sleep,' he said shortly. 'You'll be safe here.'

Rand woke to pale dawn. The fire was a mass of glowing embers and grey ash. Rolling out of his blanket, he got to his feet, kicked the fire alive, put on more brushwood until it was blazing fiercely, set the water to boil for the coffee, then tended to his mount. Meston still slept under the other blanket.

Rand studied him closely for a long while. Even asleep, there was something about the other man that stopped him cold. This man Thorpe who had hired him as scout for the wagon train had picked a gunfighter for the job, he decided. Meston had the look of a killer about him now that he was able to see the other clearly for the first time. He shook the other awake a few minutes later. Meston rolled over in the blanket, then came awake at once, jerking himself instantly upright.

Rand indicated the coffee. 'Better get some of that down you,' he advised. 'It'll help to chase away some of the chill.'

'Thanks.' The other drank the hot coffee in quick, noisy gulps. Breakfast was cooked and eaten in silence. Rand had the unshakeable feeling that the other was watching him every minute, studying him closely. He tried not to give the impression that he was aware of this scrutiny.

'You still goin' to ride on into Willard Flats?'

Rand nodded, got to his feet, went over to his mount

and tightened the cinch under the horse's belly. 'Guess I'll stick with this trail and see where it leads me,' he affirmed. 'You can either ride on east, or ride back with me. Suit yourself.'

The other pondered the alternatives for a long moment, then gave a brief nod. 'Guess I'll ride on back with you,' he said surprisingly. 'This could be kind of interestin'.'

'And if the Sutton crew catches up with you again?' Rand lifted his brows a little. 'Mebbe they won't be so slack as to use a frayed riata the next time.'

'Could be. But I'm ready for 'em this time. They got the drop on us then.'

Folding his blanket, Rand placed it on the saddle, went back to the fire and kicked dirt on to it. Stepping up into the saddle, he sat for a moment, looking down at the other. The night's rest seemed to have done him good. He was no longer tired-looking, and although his ragged clothing and the marks on his neck were still outward signs of what had happened to him, he mounted up with a swift, agile movement.

They rode over the dusty, rocky bowl of the canyon, turned a sharp corner in the trail and put the camp behind them. Once in some distant past, three rivers had flowed down the hillside. One was now the creek near where they had camped. The other two had long since dried up and there were only the beds cut through the dry rock. They travelled along one of these, moving slowly and carefully where islands of rock stood out in front of them, tall upthrusting columns which they had to circle cautiously. At the first convenient spot, they left the narrow, step-walled depression and turned right, cutting down through a long wrinkle in the ground which eventually led them to the main trail that wandered along the floor of the valley.

'How far is it to Willard Flats?' Rand asked, turning to face the other.

'Ten miles maybe.' Meston pointed. 'Just beyond that

range of hills. There's a pass leading through them.' He looked again at Rand with a swift, sharpened interest. Almost, he seemed on the point of speaking further, then he shrugged his shoulders, turned a little in the saddle, remained silent.

As the sun lifted from the eastern horizon and began to burn hotly on their backs they went along the trail with less caution, making better progress. At times, when the trail's twistings took them close to the edge of the tall timber which bordered it on both sides, Rand was able to see through clearings in the trees and make out one or other of the tall, hill pastures, stretches of lush green grass, and beyond them, tall summits, craggy rocks that lifted sheer to the cloudless heavens. The trail grew broader and smoother and presently it became a road that led up to a broad pass through the hills.

On the other side, as they rode out into more open country, he saw Willard Flats for the first time. The town lay near a bend in a sluggish river that wound around it from north to south, the water glinting brilliantly in the morning sunlight. A triple row of buildings stood on one side of the main streets that ran straight through the town. On the other side, there was a single row of tall, mainly two-storied structures. For a moment, the lay-out of the town looked so odd, so different from any that he had ever seen before, he found himself staring down at it in mild surprise.

Meston caught the look on his face, grinned mirthlessly.

'Once we get there you'll soon find out the reason for the segregation of the town. That street is the dividing line in more ways than one.'

They continued forward. A broad, wooden bridge led them across the river and a few minutes later, they were riding down the main street of Willard Flats.

'Looks quiet,' Rand remarked, letting his gaze wander along the street, eyeing the fronts of the stores and shops that stretched along one side.

'Daytime, it mostly is,' affirmed the other grimly. 'Livens up a lot at night though. That's mostly when the trouble starts.'

His interest lifting by sharp degrees, prompted by things he could both see and feel, Rand noticed the tiny groups of men, half-hidden by the deep overhang of balconies on the one side of the street. He could feel the drill of their eyes in his back, watching him as he walked forward, his own gaze glancing swiftly from right to left, eyes never still. Tension seemed to crackle on the faint breeze that soughed along the street, lifting tiny whorls of grey dust and sending them spinning along the road. He felt a tiny quiver in his limbs, set his teeth more tightly in his head.

A wagon and four came around the far end of the road, at the very edge of town, drove towards them, kicking up a cloud of dust. Rand slowed his mount to a walk. The wagon stopped in front of one of the saloons and a tall, florid-faced man climbed down from the buckboard. He was dressed entirely in black, a long frock-coat reaching almost to his knees. He stood for a moment on the slatted boardwalk, staring across the sunlit street at Rand and his companion. There was no emotion in the cold eyes, no flicker of feeling on the cruel, handsome features as the other locked his gaze with Rand's. Deliberately then, the man fished a large gold pocket-watch from his waistcoat, glanced down at it, then thrust it back, stared momentarily up at the glaring disc of the sun as if making certain that it was keeping the correct time as shown by his watch, then moved away, stepping towards the swing doors of the saloon.

He paused as he reached them, spoke in low tones to a handful of men lounging there. Rand noticed instantly how they came alert immediately, jerking upright as the other addressed them. Then the group broke up as the tall man stepped into the saloon, the doors swinging shut behind him. Two men made their way to where their mounts were tethered, stepped up into the saddle and rode quickly out of town. Neither gave Rand a single glance. It was almost as though they had forgotten his presence there. Only the fact that they had made this apparent unconcern too deliberate, heightened the faint feeling of apprehension in his mind, sending a little quiver through him.

'Like I told you, Kelsey, this is one hell of a town,' murmured Meston in a low tone.

Rand nodded. Almost, it was as if he had not heard the other. Then he said tautly: 'Who was that *hombre?*'

'Jeb Sutton.' His face was tight. 'He owns the town. Leastways, he owns that half of it.' He moved an arm to embrace the hotels, saloons and the handful of stores that lined one side of the street. He kept the faint, tightlipped smile on his face as he talked. It was a hard, bitter, thin-drawn smile and there was no hint of mirth in it. A frosty thing, Rand decided, like March in Wyoming.

He let his glance wander along the street. At first sight, it had looked no different from a hundred other similar places he had visited, frontier towns, sprawling in desert or valley, a huddle of buildings hurriedly thrown up by the pioneers, men with a deep hunger in them, anxious to expand and burst out of the narrow, encircling towns of the eastern strip. They had asked themselves neither if this was the right place to build, nor for help in building the town. They had been the first, then close on their heels had come the killers, the gamblers and crooked lawmen, the hell-on-wheels vice dens, the saloons, gunhawks and paid killers, paid by the ruthless men who moved in to grab for themselves a goodly slice of this new country which was rapidly being opened up. This was how it was with a hundred different towns along the new frontier with California.

Yet here, he was forced to admit, it was different. The ways of violence never changed, never altered, only the backgrounds and circumstances against which they were set. In most towns, the main street was the thoroughfare along which all of the traffic flowed. Stages and herds of cattle on their way to the railheads used it. It brought dangers or prosperity to a town, was indeed its lifeline.

But in Willard Flats it was something much more than that. It was the dividing line, splitting the town in two. Rand saw it all now in a single, all-encompassing glance. The veiled hints which Meston had given him made sense now that he could see it all for himself. Saloons, gambling dens, dance halls, all on the one side of the street and all owned by Jeb Sutton; stores, bank, shops, livery stables, on the other. The townfolk of Willard Flats were divided into two distinct factions, each facing the other across the main street. It was, he guessed, a situation where for a man to step across the street on to the other side, could be sufficient to precipitate a shooting battle.

He found the sheriff's office on the town side of the street, reined his mount in front of the low, wooden-roofed building with the dusty windows throwing back the glinting rays of the sun. Getting down, he rubbed his thighs to ease the shooting pains of cramp from being too long in the saddle. Meston remained seated, made no move to alight.

'You goin' inside?' Rand asked.

Meston made to shake his head, then changed his mind, shrugged his shoulders and got down, tying his horse to the hitching rail. From the story which the other had told him, there seemed little doubt that the sheriff of Willard Flats was in cahoots with Sutton, probably getting his cut of any money they managed to extract from the wagon trains passing through the town. It was also likely that his job as sheriff was safe only so long as he did as he was told by Sutton, whether he liked that set-up or not.

Sheriff Matt Blane was a short, bald-headed man with a shrewd face and narrowed, gimlet eyes that surveyed the two men standing in front of his desk with a look of suspicion. For a moment, his eyes rested on Rand, then flicked towards Meston and there was an instant look of recognition in them. He said through his teeth: 'You back in town, Meston? I figured you'd be still runnin' after what happened.'

Meston drew his brows together. 'Could be I decided there was a private score to settle with Sutton. I noticed too that you were conveniently out of town when this happened, even though you'd made it clear that we were to pay those charges put to us by Sutton.'

The other spread his hands flat on top of the desk. 'You don't expect me to be around here every day of the week, do you? I got other chores to take care of running this town and on that particular day I was out with a posse checking on some rustlers said to be hidin' out in the hills.'

'Mighty convenient for you,' sneered the other. 'Means you don't have any of those murders on your conscience, I suppose.' There was a deliberate harshness to the other's tone and he leaned forward a little, resting his knuckles on the desk.

'Now stop that talk, Meston. Count yourself lucky you're still alive.' He uttered a sharp, hoarse laugh. 'Ain't every man who cheats death like you did. Why not scoop the winnings while your luck holds? Next time you may not be so lucky.' His glance strayed back to Rand. 'Where'd you pick this jasper up, mister?'

'He rode into my camp out in the hills last night,' Rand said, watching the other carefully. Blane seemed curiously unconcerned about Meston's presence in the town, although that could have been just a front, put on until he had the chance to slip across the street and warn Sutton. Funny though, Rand reflected, Sutton had apparently not recognized the other when they had ridden into town. Unless he, too, was biding his time until the moment was ripe, and certainly Sutton had sent two of his men hightailing it back along the trail on some mission.

Suspicion, however, still lay in the tiny office. Blane searched Rand with a glance that believed nothing. 'You seem to be new around here too.'

'That's right. Rode across the alkali flats yesterday.' Leaning forward, resting his hands on the desk, he went on: 'I passed a small homestead just this side of the desert. You know it, Sheriff?'

Was it a trick of the light streaming in through the dusty window overlooking the street, or did he really see a faint fleeting look of alarm at the back of the lawman's eyes? If it was there, it was gone almost at once. Blane narrowed his gaze a little, pondered the question in his mind as if trying to place the situation. Then he said slowly: 'Sure I know it. Fellow named Jessup farms there.'

'He doesn't any longer,' Rand said grimly. 'He's dead. Shot in the back, his wife too, and the place burned down around them.'

'You sure of this?' Blane sat forward on the very edge of his chair.

'As sure as I'll ever be of anything,' said Rand tonelessly. 'I went inside to take a look around, found the two of them lying in one of the upstairs rooms. Whoever did it, couldn't have been more'n an hour ahead of me on the trail back this way. The place was still smouldering when I rode up.'

'It was Sutton and his crew,' broke in Meston savagely. 'He always swore he would finish Jessup.'

'Now just hold on there, Meston,' said Blane warningly. 'Better not start shooting off your mouth that way while you're in town. I don't want any more trouble in Willard Flats.'

'Then go tell that to Sutton,' snapped the other. 'Because if I get a chance of drawing a bead on that hombre, I'll—'

'You'll do nothing, Meston.' Blane rose to his feet sharply. 'Any more of these threats and I'll have to lock you up.'

'Sure. Then step across to the other side of the street and tell Sutton I'm here, safe inside the jail. He'll know just how to take care of things then, won't he?' He stopped, gave the idea some thought, then turned on his heel, walked over to the door, opened it carefully, and looked out along the street in both directions, running his gaze over the row of buildings on the far side of the road. Finally, he seemed satisfied that there was no immediate danger from that source, although he still appeared troubled as he turned back to the sheriff. But Blane had lost interest in him for the time being, seemed more concerned with Rand.

'You got some business here in Willard Flats, mister?' he asked tersely.

'I don't know yet.'

'What sort of answer is that?' demanded the other. 'It just turns back on itself and means nothing.'

'Do you always ask questions like this of strangers who ride into town peaceably?' Rand asked, turning the question on the other.

'Depends on what sort of men they are – and who they come riding into town with,' countered the other narrowly. 'My job is to keep law and order here in Willard Flats. I like to know why a man comes here, specially if he's totin' guns and looks as though he knows how to use 'em.' His gaze dropped meaningfully to the Colts at Rand's waist. Then he looked up again, sudden suspicion flaring in his close-set eyes. 'How do I know that you didn't shoot Jessup and his wife in the back? You could've fired the place to make it look as if Indians had done the job.'

'You don't know,' said the other harshly. He turned, moved towards the street door. 'But from what I've heard and seen, there are plenty of jaspers in this town who could have done a deed like that. This place has got a feel to it like no other place I know.'

'Better ride on out then,' advised Blane bluntly. 'Everybody coming here is watched closely. First wrong move they make could be their last.'

'If that's a threat, Sheriff, I don't take too kindly to it,' Rand shot at him.

Blane shook his head slowly. He seemed to back down a little under the other man's steady stare. 'Not a threat. Just a friendly warning. This town is like a powder keg with a slow-burnin' fuse. Sooner or later, something is goin' to

happen and it will blow up in our faces. I don't want
anything like that to happen while I'm sheriff.'

Rand gave a brief nod. Going out, he took his mount
along to the livery stables, conscious of the looks that
followed him. A handful of women, seated on a wide
balcony on the second floor of a dance hall on the other
side of the street, their painted faces looking oddly white
in the bright sunlight, gave him a speculative attention as
he passed them. Everyone looking to see how he would
line himself up now that he was in town, he thought
inwardly. He turned abruptly into the soft dimness of the
livery stable. The sweet smell of the hay was pleasant after
the dry, mouth-clogging scent of the dust from the street
and it was cool inside the long building. Handing his
mount over to the groom with instructions as to its feed
and water, he walked back to the entrance, stood with his
shoulders against one of the wooden beams. He rolled
himself a smoke, not because he felt any particular need
for one, but a smoke enabled a man to stand and watch
anything that went on in the street without appearing to
be too interested.

Casually, he let his glance wander over the people on
the sidewalks, noticing how no one seemed to cross the
road from one side to the other. He pondered the situation for a while. It was almost as if there was an invisible
barrier there making movement in that direction impossible.

He felt a momentary uneasiness flow through him. This
was a town where no man, it seemed, could afford to take
a middle course. He would be forced to line himself up
with one side or the other if he intended to stay around
for any length of time.

The groom drifted out of the rear of the stables, eyed
him up and down for a moment, evidently unsure of him.
He was an old man, eyes as bright as a bird's. Twisting a
smoke between his fingers, he said: 'You set on working
for Jeb Sutton?' He made it a hopeful question.

Rand thinned his lips. Then he shook his head slowly.

The other leaned forward, waiting for his answer. 'No,' he said finally. 'I'm working for nobody right now. Just want to get myself a room in one of the hotels here. Heard there was land to be had round here, thought I might ride over and look some of it over, see if it's right for me.'

'Land?' The other teetered on one leg for a moment, then struck a sulphur match and applied the flame to the end of the cigarette. He drew in a deep breath.

'Well, isn't there?'

The groom shrugged. 'Reckon that's so. About twenty miles west of here. But you don't look the sort of *hombre* to settle down and become a nester. Or maybe you're set on findin' gold?' The other's eyes narrowed a little.

'If I like this place, I may settle down here permanently. So far, I haven't seen much in this town that I like. It's a hell of a place. Everybody walking around waiting for the other side to make a wrong move.'

'You rode into town with Meston, didn't you?' The old man's glance met his own head-on.

'That's right. Found him out on the trail. Told me quite a story about this town. It wasn't very pleasant.'

'If you'd seen as much as I have, you'd ride on out of here and never come back.' The other sucked in his cheeks, let smoke trickle out through his nostrils.

'What sort of things?' Rand asked quietly. He had almost finished his smoke, dropped the butt on to the dust and ground it in with his heel.

The other shrugged, changed the subject swiftly and adroitly. 'If you want a good hotel on this side of the street, there's only one. Hard by the bank yonder.' He pointed a bony finger.

Rand moved away. Behind him, he heard the other's dry, hard chuckle, half-wise and half-foolish and thought: He knows I'm not here to buy land or look for gold.

He made his way along the boardwalk, stopped for a moment in front of the hotel. Then he pushed open the doors and stepped inside. Signing the register, he took the key to his room, climbed the twisting stairs, went into the small room that overlooked the street, locked the door behind him, and laid his gear out on the bed. There was a basin and a bowl of cold water on the bureau near the window, and taking off his shirt, he washed his face, rubbing it well with soap to remove the last traces of dust. Slipping his shirt back on, he drank his fill from what water was left, then went down to the dining room. It was almost noon and he did not have long to wait for a meal. As he ate, he wondered about Meston, what the other had had to talk over with the Sheriff after he had left them. There had been little sense in the other trying to make any official complaint of what had happened. Blane would do nothing that went against Sutton and the chances were that Meston would find himself on the run once more. Well, that was his look out, he decided. He had not come here to be nursemaid to men like that.

Remaining at his table after he had finished eating, he built himself a smoke, leaned back in his chair, enjoying the chance to relax. There were a few other diners in the room. Most of them were ordinary looking men, clerks, storekeepers. Naturally there would be none of the men from the other side of the street, he reflected. They would stick to their own yard, stay there until something happened that would start guns talking along the main street of Willard Flats.

He drew deeply on the cigarette, watched the tip glow redly, staring down at it as the thin spiral of smoke drifted bluely towards the ceiling. There was a sudden movement in the doorway and he glanced up as three men entered. They paused there, looking about them, and a moment later, Rand saw the desk clerk crowd in at their backs. Rand saw the other's gaze drift over the room until it rested on him. Then the clerk bent and said something to the portly, bewhiskered man in the black frock coat standing a little in front of the other two men, similarly attired.

The portly man nodded, then led the way to Rand's table, paused in front of it, then said quietly: 'Mind if we have a word with you, Mister Kelsey?'

Rand looked up at him in mild surprise, then shook his head, nodded towards the other chairs at the table. 'Sit down, gentlemen,' he said. 'You seem to know who I am, anyway.'

'Got your name from the desk clerk,' said the first man. He lowered his tone a little. 'My name is Merriam, Clive Merriam. I own the bank in town. These are Jess Blake and Hal Foster, both store-owners.'

Rand nodded to the others, turned his attention back to Merriam. 'What is it you want to talk to me about?'

The other rested his back against the chair, let his hands hang loosely on the edge of the table. He eyed Rand speculatively for a long moment as if trying to make up his mind about the other. Then he said softly: 'Don't let this town fool you, mister. You can see how it is now, even though you've only been here for an hour or so.'

'I can see that there could be trouble brewing here at any minute with the set-up you've got in Willard Flats,' Rand said evenly. 'A man seems to be on one side or on the other, with no in-betweens.'

'That's just how it is.' The other relaxed abruptly as though he had just been under some kind of strain. Patting the pocket of his coat, he dug into it and brought out a thick cigar, lit it and thrust it between his lips. He seemed to have gained some of his normal reassurance. Closing his eyes for a moment, he sat forward, then opened them again to study Rand, keenly and sharply.

'We noticed the way you came over to this side once you left the sheriff's office. That prompted us to come along and have a talk with you. No doubt you've heard of Jeb Sutton. He owns the other side of the street, brings in all of the undesirables, gamblers, gunmen. Sooner or later, if he's allowed to continue this way unchecked, the whole town will come under his reign of terror and it won't be a place for decent men and women to live in. We're trying to stop that and we've had a limited amount of success, but we're having to fight hardened gunmen and that isn't easy.'

'We?' Rand prompted.

'The Vigilante Committee. When it was clear that Sutton and his gunmen would ride roughshod over the town if we didn't do something about it, we set up a Vigilante Movement to protect our own interests. We need every man we can get if we're to put a stop to this senseless killing and outlawry.'

'Are you offerin' me a job?' said Rand keenly.

The other pursed his lips, made to go on but at that moment, Blake butted in sharply. 'We need men who know how to handle guns. Most of us are just ordinary storekeepers. We've had no cause to learn how to shoot fast and quick, how to kill. Sutton is only biding his time. When he judges that the hour is right, he'll turn his gunwolves loose on us. Where do you reckon we'll be then?'

'I can see your point,' Rand conceded. 'But this is no quarrel of mine. I just rode in here to look over the place, see if it's the right sort of town in which to settle down, or whether I ought to ride on and find some other place.'

'Then you won't help us in this fight?' said the other flatly.

'I'd like to know a little more of what's goin' on around these parts before I throw in my lot with either side.'

'If you decide to join forces with Sutton, then you may well regret it,' said Foster quietly. There was something very bright and calculating at the back of his eyes; something that Rand could not quite decipher.

'Why do you say that?'

'Because sooner or later, the law is goin' to catch up with him and the killers who ride with him. He reckons he's safe so long as he stays on the other side of the street, so long as he has Blane in with him, and that pack of gunwolves running at his back. But there'll come a time when real law and order comes to Willard Flats and then there'll be no place for the likes of him. This country is expanding west now and we'll soon be a frontier town no longer. If the railroad comes through here, that day will come sooner than most people reckon.'

'And in the meantime?' asked Rand smoothly.

'We've petitioned the Governor to send men to help us. So far we've had no one unless—' He broke off as a sudden thought seemed to strike him.

Rand said in a half-interested manner. 'Unless what?'

'Nothing,' said the other shortly. He shook his head as if angry at himself for having said more than he intended. Rand guessed that there had been something in the other's mind which had prompted his earlier remark, wondered what it was.

Merriam leaned forward, holding the half-smoked cigar between his fingers. 'Then you won't throw in your lot with us, Kelsey?'

'I said I'll think about it. Right now, I don't intend to get caught up in a fight like this.'

The three men paused for a moment, then got to their feet, scraping back their chairs. Merriam said coldly: 'If you should change your mind, we'll be around someplace. But don't take too long. There's no place here for a man who tries to ride a middle trail. Sooner or later, he winds up dead.'

THREE

DEAD MEN'S TALES

Even at that early hour of the morning, the sun was blistering hot and it shone through the window of his room, directly on to his upturned face. Rand Kelsey rolled over in the low bed, kept his eyes tightly closed and tried to shut the sun out of his eyes, but it was impossible to do so and in the end he gave it up, thrust himself up on to his hand, then swung his legs to the floor and stood up. After a second or so, he blinked his eyes several times against the glare, went over to the basin and splashed water on to his face and neck, used the towel gingerly. His skin was still scorched from that long ride over the desert.

As he pulled on his shirt, he recalled the meeting the previous day with the three citizens of Willard Flats. From what he had already seen of this place, he did not doubt that the vigilantes were getting the worst of the fighting. He did not know how many guns they had, but he could guess that they would not fight as well as men who had been paid to do it, wanted men on the run from the law in a dozen states, who knew that they were safe here only so long as Sutton protected them.

Going downstairs into the dining room, he ate his breakfast in a leisurely manner, washed it down with a couple of cups of strong, black coffee, smoked a cigarette, then went out into the street. The heat struck him almost

45

at once with the force of a physical blow. The wind was blowing straight off the desert to the east, he reckoned, bringing with it all of the terrible, blistering heat of that place. At certain times of the year, this would happen, when the prevailing winds came from that particular direction and there would be drought and heat in the town.

He spotted the portly figure of Merriam, the banker, directly ahead of him on the boardwalk. The other had turned, seen him come out of the hotel and now stood waiting for him. As Rand came up to him the other pulled out a large red handkerchief, mopped his brow with it. Perspiration formed a thin, shining film on his flabby-jowled features.

'You thought over my proposition, Mister Kelsey?' he asked.

Rand pursed his lips, shook his head. 'I figure I'll just stay around and look at things from the middle for a while,' he replied.

The other narrowed his eyes a little, and his thick lips were pressed more tightly together. 'You could be making a big mistake,' he said warningly. His glance passed over Rand's shoulder, as he looked quickly to the other side of the street. Rand turned his head casually, noticed the small group of men who had just come out of the saloon directly opposite them. They grinned sneeringly as they saw Rand and the banker watching them.

'By that remark, I suppose you mean there's a chance I'll get caught in the crossfire when it comes to a show-down.'

'Perhaps.' The banker thrust the handkerchief back into his pocket, looked up at Rand for a long moment, then turned on his heel and hurried into the bank. Rand stared after him for a moment, then walked on. The group of men were no longer on the opposite sidewalk he noticed. While he and Merriam had been speaking, they had gone back into the saloon.

He went along to the livery stable, checked on his

mount, then acting on impulse, walked deliberately across the street, his spurs raking up little clouds of dust be hind him. Shoving the saloon's door open with the flat of his hand, he went inside, crossed over to the bar and stood with his elbows on it, resting his weight on them. Seven other men were inside this saloon. One of them was standing close to the wall, near the window that looked out on to the street. He turned his head and eyed Rand with a look of frank curiosity as the other stood at the bar. Then he pushed himself away from the wall and came over, standing close to him.

The barkeep moved forward. There seemed to be a look of apprehension on his grey-pasty features.

'Whiskey,' Rand said quietly. He tossed a coin on to the bar.

The barkeep stared down at the spinning coin as though mesmerized by it. His face was drained of all emotion. Then his glance lifted to Rand's face for a moment before sliding away to look at the other man close by.

'You walked here from the other side of the street, stranger,' said the man beside Rand.

'That's right,' Rand answered evenly. 'Didn't know there was a law in town against that.'

'Seems to me there's a whole heap of things you don't know,' went on the other softly. 'You could be a stranger in town, I suppose. On the other hand you may have done that deliberately just to start something. I saw you talking with Merriam a few moments ago. Seemed to be having quite an earnest little discussion. Did he pay you to come over here and force a showdown? If he did, then you can go right back there and tell him we're ready any time he likes to make his play, maybe that we'll start it ourselves. '

'I don't know what you're talking about,' Rand said calmly. 'I came here for a drink. There's my money on the bar.' He nodded towards the coin resting in front of him.

The man regarded him curiously for a long moment, the pale-grey eyes not once leaving the other's face. Then

he said tightly. 'Give him his drink, Phil. If he is tryin'
somethin', he won't walk out of here alive. Maybe we
should let him have one last drink.'

There was a round of coarse laughter from the other
men seated at a couple of tables, a few feet away.

Rand grinned tightly. 'You talk too much, my friend,'
he said, his voice very soft.

The smile went from the other man's face. He stepped
back a couple of paces. 'So you did come in here lookin'
for trouble,' he said harshly.

Rand had no illusions as to what the other's intentions
were at that moment. The man was spoiling for a fight and
whether it was to be with fists or guns, was of little conse-
quence to him.

'Like I told you. I came here for a drink. If you want to
make anything more out of it than that then you're at
liberty to do so.'

The other smiled again, a deliberately sneering smile.
'It disturbs me, stranger,' he murmured, 'having a ranny
from the other side comin' in here and tryin' to drink with
men.'

'You're too sensitive,' Rand's tone was deliberately
provocative. 'Point is, who's goin' to stop me drinking?'

The smile on the other's face froze instantly as Rand
turned away from the counter to face him directly. 'I'll do
it,' he said thickly.

Rand nodded. 'Make your play,' he said quietly. There
was not the slightest trace of emotion in his voice. He eyed
the other closely, not watching the man's hand as it
hovered close above the gun in his belt, but keeping a
close watch on his eyes, for it was there that the danger
signal would come. The gunman's hand trembled above
his Colt for a few seconds as if he were plucking up the
necessary courage to face this gunman whose calibre he
did not know. Then his jaw muscles tightened abruptly
and in that same moment his right hand flashed down for
the gun in its holster. Still Rand's hand had not made a
move. The other's gun was almost clear of leather before

Rand's band jerked down and the ranny found himself staring into the round circular black hole of Rand's Colt before he could jerk his own weapon clear of leather.

Even as he stared down as though mesmerised by the speed of the other man's draw, Rand's thumb moved slowly and there was an ominous click which lashed across the taut silence in the room as the hammer was thumbed back, the weapon cocked.

The gun in Rand's hand was held stone steady, lined up on the other's chest. He said thinly through gritted teeth. 'I could shoot you down right there, mister, and I'd have every right to do it.'

'Then why don't you go ahead?' snarled the other harshly. 'Maybe you're scared of what Jeb Sutton might do if he came along and found that you'd shot down one of his men. Remember the only witnesses in this place, or on this side of the street will testify against you.'

'But you won't be here to see it,' Rand told him, his tone ominous.

There was no reply from the other. His face had paled as he realized that death stood only a few short feet away from him and it needed only the slightest pressure on the trigger to blast him into eternity.

'Go ahead.' The other's throat muscles worked convulsively as he spoke.

Rand shook his head. 'Killers like you need a special lesson. Unbuckle that gunbelt and let it drop.'

The gunhawk's eyes widened. He licked his lips nervously, let his glance flick towards the rest of the men, seated at the table. Dryly, Rand said: 'Don't expect any help from them. The first wrong move they make will be their last and they know it.'

'You intend to shoot me down in cold blood?' muttered the other.

'Drop that gunbelt and I'll show you what I mean to do.'

Hesitantly, the other unbuckled the heavy belt. For a moment, the thought of trying to make a snatch for his gun, to beat Rand to the draw, lived in his eyes, then he evidently decided against it, let the belt fall with a clatter on to the floor.

'Step back a couple of paces,' Rand ordered, moving forward. As the other obeyed, he deliberately hooked his boot around the gunbelt and sent it flying into the far corner of the room. Then he thrust his own gun back into its holster, said thinly through tightly-clenched teeth. 'Now we'll see what you can do with your fists.'

A crafty look crept into the other's eyes and a tight smile spread over his features. He gave a quick nod. He was a big man, a solid shape, scarred by trouble and hungering for more now that the odds were evened. Along the trail, Rand had met many like him, narrow of mind, governed by passion and the burning desire to hurt, maim and kill.

There was a dull shine in his eyes as he moved forward, balanced evenly on the balls of his feet, huge fists cocked ready to hammer his opponent to a bloody pulp. He squared himself at Rand as he edged forward, began to say something harshly through his teeth, but Rand was not listening. It was an old trick this, muttering words that could not be made out in an attempt to distract one's attention from what he really meant to do. He would be a dirty fighter, Rand decided, keeping his eyes on the man's face, one who knew most of the tricks in the book, and some others besides. He would not stop fighting until he had either smashed Rand down, or been beaten senseless himself.

Abruptly, he swung his right fist all the way up from his belt. Had it connected on its intended target, it would have finished the fight there and then, but Rand was ready for him, had guessed what was coming and the other's ham-like fist connected with nothing more solid than empty air, sailing over the other's shoulder as he bobbed easily away from the blow. Off-balance, the other fell heavily against Rand and instantly, he caught at him around the waist, tightening his hold savagely, bearing him back against the bar. His head struck Rand hard under the chin, jerking his head back, with a blow that sent pain roaring through his skull. He kept himself upright with a tremendous effort, hooked one leg behind the gunman's ankle, hauled back swiftly with his foot, seeking to throw the man off balance, knowing what would be coming next. His swift, twisting motion took the other completely by surprise and the knee which had been aimed for his groin, struck the hard woodwork of the bar instead.

Howling harshly with pain and anger, the man fell back, releasing his tight hold around Rand's waist. Swiftly, he sucked down a gust of air, shook his head in an attempt to clear it of the throbbing ache that hammered through it, then turned to face the other as he came lunging forward with an animal-like bellow of rage. He swung two wild blows at Rand's head. The first missed completely and the second grazed along his cheek, drawing blood as the other's iron-hard knuckles scraped his flesh. The side of his head seemed on fire as he rolled with the blow.

The moment he did so, he knew that he had made a mistake. He had deliberately kept the other gunhawks at the tables in front of him where he could keep an eye on them, although he had not expected them to try to make any trouble or interfere in the fight unless it was obvious that it was going against their companion.

But he had completely forgotten about the barkeep at his back. Evidently the man had decided that he ought to get in on the fight, probably to keep well in with Sutton. The blow which the barkeep aimed at him took him on the side of the head. For a moment, he felt his senses leave him and his knees buckled under him as though no longer able to bear his weight. There was a dull thumping in his head and the room seemed to dim in front of his vision. Desperately, he fought to cover up as the gunman came in with a shout of triumph. He had moved away from the bar instinctively the moment that first blow had been struck from behind. Now he was no longer within reach of the barkeep, but the gunhawk was circling around him, his face dimly seen through the red haze that hovered in front of Rand's stultified vision. His lips were twisted back revealing uneven teeth as a snarling grin of hungry triumph showed on his mouth. A hammer-like blow struck Rand in the chest, almost caving in his ribs and he felt his breath whoosh from his lungs in a hard, explosive gasp.

'This is the finish for you, cowboy,' hissed the other. 'I'll teach you to pull a gun on Cal Colter.'

Rand used his arms and elbows to nullify the full fury of the other's blows. His vision was beginning to clear slowly, Colter's face swam back into focus. He aimed a sudden blow at it, caught the other flush on the chin, sending him reeling back. There was still not the full force of his strength behind the blow, but sufficient to make the man more wary. He came crowding in, arms flailing. Side-stepping the blows which the other rained on him, Rand threw two more punches to Colter's face, felt a keen sense of satisfaction as his knuckles hit hard on the man's nose, reducing it to a bloody pulp. Cartilage gave under the fury of that blow and Colter staggered back, yelling loudly. For a moment he stood there, absolutely motionless, staring down at the blood smeared on the back of the hand he had put up to his nose.

Rand hit him low in the solar plexus. The man wilted, bent forward, buckling at the knees, arms hanging limply by his sides and at that moment, Rand brought the side of his stiffened hand down on the man's neck, hitting him just behind the left ear. The other slid to the floor without uttering a single sound, lay in a curled heap at Rand's feet. He stood away from the unconscious man. His face burned from the force of those earlier blows and there was a dull, aching pain in the side of his chest, and each breath he drew down sent a stab of agony through him. He moved towards the bar, one hand close to his waist.

'I've got a good mind to shoot you down,' he said through his teeth to the barkeep. 'That wasn't a sensible thing to do.'

The man's face was drained of all colour, had taken on a pasty look and he deliberately held his hands flat on the bar in front of him where Rand could see, palms down.

'I – I wasn't tryin' to—' He broke off, glanced up with relief at a sudden movement at the door. Rand turned slowly, rubbing his chin with his fingers. He recognized Jeb Sutton at once as the man came into the bar, with three of his crew at his back. Sutton advanced into the centre of the room and stood staring down at Colter, lying on the floor near one of the tables. There was a curious expression on his face. Then he lifted his head and laid his gaze on Rand.

'What happened here?' he asked quietly.

'Seems he didn't like me drinkin' in this saloon,' Rand said. 'We had a little argument and—'

'This *hombre* started it all, boss,' broke in one of the men at the nearest table. 'Came in here from the other side, like a stray dog with his tail high.'

'That right?' asked Sutton softly. 'Seems I recollect seeing your face before.' He wrinkled his brow in thought for a moment, then nodded. 'That's right. You rode into town yesterday with Meston.'

Rand noticed the expressions on the faces of the rest of the men, saw them glance at each other, but it was impossible to read anything from their faces.

Rand turned his back on the others, looked hard at the barkeep. Sutton and the men with him exchanged glances, then the tall, hard-faced man said: 'It's all right, let him have his drink.'

'Sutton,' said Rand after a spell, finishing his drink before he spoke. 'It seems to me that you're not too sure of yourself, even now when you seem to have this whole town sewn up real tight. You're afraid that the Vigilantes might gain more support and give you the fight of your life.'

'What makes you think I can't win that fight?' muttered the other, leaning on the bar a few feet away. Sutton took the bottle from the counter and poured himself a drink, threw it over in a quick gulp, grimacing a little as the raw liquor hit the back of his throat.

'Maybe you can,' agreed Rand softly. 'But there's always

the chance that before that happens, there may be men ridin' in here, sent by the Governor in response to the appeal these men have sent to him. If that happens, then there may be troops or Federal marshals here and you won't be able to deal with them so easily.'

Sutton shrugged seemingly unconcerned at that prospect. 'I figure that pretty soon, these so-called Vigilantes will be finished. I've got enough men here to finish them now but I prefer to bide my time.'

'When do you figure on makin' your move then?' Rand did not turn his head as he asked the question, was apparently looking casually down into the empty glass in his hands.

'That's something I've still got to decide.' The other did not intend to be drawn on this question, and certainly not by a stranger who had walked over from the other side of the street. 'Are you lookin' for a job?'

'Riding or fighting?' Rand asked pointedly.

'Could be more of one than the other,' replied Sutton evenly. He poured another drink, sipped this one more slowly as if determined to savour the taste of the whiskey this time. 'I need men who are handy with their gun and' – he glanced down at the unconscious Colter as if to add more meaning to his next words – 'and their fists.'

'Now that's the second offer of that kind I've had since I rode into town,' said Rand. 'Seems to me this whole town is goin' to bust loose at the seams any minute and both sides are doin' their best to hire as many guns as possible before it happens. '

Sutton's eyes narrowed. Rand saw the flare of temper beginning in his face, but he fought it down, bringing it sharply under tight control. 'So those other critters also approached you on the same subject?'

'That's right. Offered me a job with them. They seem determined to run you out of town, Sutton.'

The other's answer was less than Rand had expected in the circumstances. 'I figure they know the consequences of that.'

'This *hombre* Meston. He claimed that you attacked the wagon train for which he was scout when they pulled out of town, killed all of the others and he managed to escape by the skin of his teeth due to a frayed riata.'

Sutton grinned and his smile was not a pleasant thing. He shrugged as though the affair was of little notice as far as he was concerned, but there was a certain forced tightness in his tone as he went on: 'Now that he's been foolish enough to ride back into town after all that has happened, he may not find it so easy to ride on back out again.'

'Then you mean to kill him?'

'I'll let him worry about that for a little while. It'll do him good to try to hide from me, never knowing when the end is going to come. A swift bullet from the darkness or maybe another rope waiting at the edge of town. He'll never know which it is to be until it actually happens.'

The streak of cruelty was showing in the other now. Rand picked up the bottle, poured a drink, then glanced round as the man on the floor began to stir. He opened his eyes, sat up and gingerly rubbed the side of his neck where Rand had hit him that last, crushing blow. Slowly, memory returned to his face and he lifted his head, saw Rand standing there in front of him and tried to claw his way to his feet, lips twisted angrily, a deep and growing hatred in his eyes.

'Hold it there, Cal,' said Sutton sharply.

The other stopped immediately, held back, but the hatred was still there and the look on his face boded ill for Rand should the other ever get him at an advantage.

'I'll remember this, stranger,' he said softly, his voice little more than a husky whisper.

Almost as if there had been no interruption, Sutton said sharply: 'Well, mister, what do you think of my offer? If you're on the run from the law, that doesn't matter in the least as far as I'm concerned. You'll be safe here so long as you do as you're told. The pay is good, free board, lodgings.'

Rand smiled faintly. He downed his drink, wiped his

mouth with the back of his hand. 'Like I told the others who made me the same offer, I'll think it over.'

Sutton drew himself fully erect at that. Clearly it was not the answer he had been expecting. Either an acceptance or a curt refusal perhaps, but not this.

'I tell you he's been sent here to spy on us,' broke in Colter thinly. He kept dabbing gingerly at his smashed nose, eyes not once leaving Rand's face and there was the look in them that one saw in a rattler's eyes before it struck at its helpless victim. 'Merriam and the others wouldn't dare step across here themselves so they sent this ranny to do their dirty work and look things over for them. Maybe they figured he was fast enough with a gun to take one or two of us with him if we forced a showdown.'

'That's enough of that kind of talk, Colter,' snapped Sutton. 'If there is any decidin' to be done here, I'll do it.' His pale gaze swept back to Rand.

'If you are in cahoots with that bunch on the other side you did a very foolish thing coming over here like you did. I could have you gunned down and nobody would stop it or say anything. But somehow, I don't think you're that stupid.' His eyes widened a little. 'Be that as it may, I can't afford to have men around town, fast men with a gun, that I can't trust, that I don't know where they stand. Either a man is with me or he's against me and there ain't no two ways about it. So I reckon that you have a choice right here and now. Either you accept my offer and join me, or you ride on out of town and keep on ridin'.'

Rand felt the whole atmosphere inside the saloon tighten abruptly at the other's words. It closed around him like a bag being drawn shut or the noose of a hempen rope being pulled into a narrowing, choking circle.

'Could be that I like this place,' he said flatly, letting his words drop into the clinging silence. His deep tones vibrated in the stillness of the room. There was no mistaking the implications of his cool statement. He saw Sutton flush, saw the veins stand out thickly on his neck, but he held himself in with a conscious effort.

It was Colter who spoke first. He said flatly: 'Could be that we have a place for *hombres* like you just outside of town.' He spoke through his teeth. 'You ain't the first to come here with a chip on his shoulder, fast with a gun, figuring on changing things.'

'Now that's mighty interestin',' said Rand. In spite of himself, in spite of the tight grip he had on his emotions, he felt a sudden, momentary tightness in his mind. 'I suppose that you shot them in the backs too. Reckon a killer like you, big with his mouth, wouldn't have the nerve to face up to such men in fair fight.' He was deliberately goading the other, wanting Colter to talk more about these other men, about one man in particular. But Sutton had realized just what it was he was trying to do and he cut in sharply. 'That's goin' to be enough of that kind of talk, I said, Colter. I won't be warnin' you again.'

'Maybe so,' muttered the other, not wanting to back down yet, still full of his fury and the pride that had turned yeasty in him when he had tried to beat Rand a few minutes earlier. 'No man faces me down.'

'If you have anythin' to settle with this man, then you'll do it someplace else,' Sutton said with authority. 'I'll have no shootin' in here.'

Colter turned unwilling eyes on the other, his face suddenly sullen, licked his lips dryly with the tip of his tongue. Then he said shortly to Rand: 'Not right now, maybe. But this matter between us ain't finished yet.'

'Any time you choose,' Rand said, very soft. 'I'll be waiting.'

Finishing his drink, he set the empty glass down on the bar, gave a swift nod to Sutton and walked towards the door.

From behind him, Sutton said: 'Remember what I told you, mister. Ride on out of town if you want to stay alive. If you're still here after sundown, my men will come shooting. This ain't exactly a friendly place as you've discovered and a man can easily step into the way of a bullet meant for somebody else.'

'Thanks for the warning. I'll take care to watch my back while I'm here.' He let the doors swing shut behind him, stepped down into the dusty, heat-filled street. There was a faint movement on the other side as he began to walk along in the direction of the livery stable. From the corner of his eye he glimpsed the tall, angular-faced Jess Blake, standing at the intersection with one of the narrower streets a short distance away. The other gave him a sharp, piercing stare and then deliberately turned on his heel and walked off into the narrow alley. Rand felt a grim amusement in him. He could guess where the other was headed at that moment, along to tell the other members of the Vigilante Committee that Rand Kelsey had been seen leaving one of the saloons on the other side of the street.

Rand Kelsey rode down the main street of Willard Flats, paused at one of the intersections and looked both ways. His horse had a loose shoe and he guessed there was a smith somewhere in this town. Not only would the other be able to put things right as far as his mount was concerned, but a blacksmith was the one man in town who would be able to give him some information that he needed badly. Most people considered a smith to be one of the more ignorant of the population, whereas in truth he knew far more of what went on in a town than perhaps the editor of the local paper. People were inclined to talk to him, tell him their troubles, where they were headed if they rode out of town and needed a shoe fixing as he did right now. Whether the other would talk to him or not, was something he did not know.

Halfway along the street, a man moved out of the shadows of the wooden overhang of one of the buildings and stepped down into the street directly in front of him. Rand reined up with a low, muttered curse, then paused as he recognized the other.

Meston put up a hand to Rand's bridle, holding it tightly in his fingers. 'Heard that you'd been spotted coming out of one of Sutton's saloons a while back, Kelsey,' he said. There was nothing in his tone, nor showing on his face, to give any indication of the thoughts going through his mind at that moment.

'So?' Rand raised his brows a shade, glanced down at the other.

'So I figure you ought to ride slow and careful around these parts. Just a friendly warning, nothing more. I know these folk.' He rubbed at his throat meaningly. 'Don't try to play one side off against the other. It won't work.'

'I'll bear that in mind.' Gigging his horse forward, Rand rode on. He did not look behind him, but he knew that Meston was watching him narrowly as he rode away, probably wondering what sort of man he was, and what kind of business would bring him here.

At the end of the block, he came upon the smithy. The smith was a squat, powerfully-built man, face glistening a little with the heat. He glanced up from the anvil on which he was pounding a horseshoe into shape. Dipping it into the tub of cold water beside the small forge, he said above the hiss of steam. 'Howdy, mister. Anything I can do for you?'

'I'd like you to take a look at his shoes. Figured one of 'em was working loose.'

'Sure. Light down and I'll have a look.' The other placed the horseshoe on the bench nearby, rubbed his hands on his leather apron. Sighing a little, he knelt and lifted the horse's leg, examined the shoe closely.

'Guess you must've been around here for some time,' Rand said casually.

The other nodded and uttered a low grunt which could have meant anything. Then he straightened. 'One of these shoes is a mite loose. If you're meanin' to ride any distance better let me fix it for you. Won't take more'n ten minutes.'

'Sure.' Rand gave a quick nod, lit a smoke and leaned his shoulders against one of the stout wooden uprights.

Speaking through the smoke that wreathed his face, he

said quietly: 'You know most of the men in this place?'

'Depends which side of the street you're talkin' about,' countered the other. 'I know most of the townsfolk, though I don't have much to do with the crew that runs around with Jeb Sutton. I fix their mounts for 'em, but that's all.'

'Did you ever know an hombre called Turner, Jim Turner? Rode into Willard Flats about six weeks ago, maybe a little before that.'

'Turner?' The other lifted his head and stared up at him for a long moment, brow wrinkled in thought. 'Can't say I ever heard that name before. Unless he was with Sutton.'

'Somehow I doubt that. He was a loner, wouldn't side with anybody. Tall, dark-haired. Rode a black stallion.'

Rand saw by the sudden look in the smith's eyes that this last piece of information had fixed Jim Turner in the other's mind. The smith gave a brisk nod. 'Now that you mention the horse he was ridin', I do remember him. Quiet fella, said he meant to make a lucky strike in the hills. Rode out of town one morning about five weeks ago and never came back.'

'Anybody know what could have happened to him?'

The smith shook his head. 'Why should you figure that anything has happened to him? Plenty of men ride out of here, lookin' for gold and they don't come back for more supplies for mebbe six months. He's probably still out there in the hills, still lookin' for gold. Not that he's likely to find any and even if he does, he won't keep it for long once he rides back into town with it. Those gamblers on the other side of the street can take a man for every grain of dust he's got in a single night. What they don't get by cheatin' at cards, they get by theft in one of the alleys after dark.'

'I figured that might be the way of things,' ruminated Rand. 'Though I doubt if he'd be the sort of man to spend his life lookin' for gold.'

'You a friend of his?' asked the other keenly.

'You might say that. Knew him in the Army. Last I heard of him he was headed this way across the desert. Got a telegraph from him eight weeks ago when he said he'd let me know how he made out here. When I didn't hear from him, I figured I'd better ride on this way for a look-see. From what I've seen of this town already, it isn't hard to see that a loner might run into bad trouble very soon after ridin' in here.'

'You could be right,' nodded the other slowly. He finished fixing the horse's shoe. The way he said it made it sound a question or a challenge of quick suspicion. 'You figure on ridin' out into the hills and takin' a look there for yourself?'

'That's right. If anythin' has happened, I mean to find out for myself.'

The smith shrugged, took the coin that Rand gave him and thrust it into the pocket of his apron. 'Those hills hold plenty of men on the run from the law,' he advised. 'They've got a reputation as a shelter for gunslingers and rustlers. You go in there and you may find yourself in even worse trouble than here in town.'

'I reckon that's a risk I'll have to take.' Rand said the words almost to himself.

'He must have been a good friend of yours for you to want to risk your neck like this just to find out what might have happened to him,' murmured the other.

'He was,' Rand told him. 'And if there has been any gunplay and I do manage to find him, I'll take this place apart to find his killer.' There was no bravado in his tone as he made this statement, merely a quiet, ominous tautness; and the smith, staring up at him as he climbed back into the saddle, felt a little shiver go through him as he caught the look on Rand's face. When he went back to the forge, pumping hard on the bellows, he found himself still thinking about the other. He did not doubt that the other had meant every word he had said.

Meanwhile, the object of the smith's thoughts was riding out of town, heading west towards the tall hills that lifted some fifteen miles or so in the distance. It was early afternoon now and the heat head lay over everything with a crushing, dehydrating pressure. It brought the sweat boiling out of his body and the sweatband of his hat left an angry red mark on his forehead.

He moved along at a slow pace, not giving in to the urgent restlessness that was bubbling up inside him. Whatever happened, he would not have to rush into this situation blindly. There was too much at stake and too many irons in the fire right now. His first mistake could easily be his last and Sutton had been close to the mark when he had said that a bullet could come from any direction.

Rubbing his forehead, he wiped the film of sweat away, screwed up his eyes against the vicious, blinding glare of sunlight. The low-roofed huts on one side of the trail leading out of town were empty. deserted. This, he guessed, was the oldest part of the town. A handful of shacks which had promised to be the start of something bigger, greater, more noble. Instead, Willard Flats had turned into this, a hell-town in which men faced each other across the narrow, dusty strip of the main street, guns in their hands, ready for all hell to be let loose at the slightest provocation.

FOUR

THE LONER

Rand Kelsey rode steadily across the vast basin that fronted the distant hills. At times, he reined up, pausing on top of some low rise to scan his backtrail, but there was no sign that he was being followed from Willard Flats and he felt a growing easiness in his mind. Around four o'clock, he found some dry leaf and used it to build himself a smokeless fire. He ate a quick meal of bacon and flapjacks, washed them down with black coffee, then climbed into the saddle again with the sun just beginning to slide down the deep blue vaults to the west. He was still five or six miles from the low foothills, but already there was a certain coolness in the breeze that blew down to him from the upper reaches of the hills.

By sundown, he was well into the hills. Here, there was a multitude of trails, narrowed and more twisting than that which had led him over the smooth floor of the wide basin. It was difficult for a man to know which trail to choose, he pondered, sitting tall in the saddle and peering about him in the growing dimness. Already, the reds and golds of the sunset were colouring the hill crests and the ground about him, adding a touch of flame to the coarse grass and the bare rocks which lifted all around him. He sat quite still, debating whether to move deeper into the hills before making camp, or to remain where he was and wait until morning before making any decision as to which trail to take.

Jim Turner could have taken any one of a dozen similar trails when he had ridden out this way, he reflected, always assuming that he had come out here. He saw no reason why the smith should lie about that, but there had been something about that town he had just left which made it difficult for a man to really believe anybody. He doubted if he would have really believed the local preacher now. There had been too many people there with too much to hide; distrustful people who had grown so used to having fear as their elbow companion and sudden death as their only heritage that they had forgotten to think clearly and straight.

He stepped down from his mount, walked it towards a small clearing on a broad shelf of level ground a little way off the trail. The deep reds were beginning to flicker back and forth across the heavens now and there was a deep tint of purple-black in them as the night came in from the east. Very soon, he knew, all of the colours would be swamped by the darkness and there would be the hazy scattering of stars over the sky above his head. This was what he really liked, living out in the open with all of that space around him and above him, with no sense of being shut in as one experienced in a room at one of the hotels in town.

This time, he did not light a fire, but ate cold beef, tearing at the tough meat with his teeth, chewing reflectively on it as he sat with his back to one of the trees and stared off into the last fading glow of the sunset. There was always something about both sunrise and sunset that did something to a man who spent most of his life on the trail. It was impossible for him to analyse his feelings and guess what it was; a sense of seeing the world at its very beginning and end, perhaps, unsullied by heat or cold, the short, brief period between glaring sunlight and cold starlight. Maybe it was because of the fact that they lasted for such a brief moment that they had this particular pull on him.

Tilting his head back a little, he stared off into the tall crests of the hills that were pointed like fingers to the darkening sky. His brows drew together as if he were looking clear through the faint mists, to where Jim Turner might be at that moment, whether he was dead or still alive. He tried to reason with himself, to discover why he felt so sure that Turner was no longer alive. It was a feeling that had been in his mind when that telegraph message from the other had become overdue and it had grown stronger with every passing mile and day since then.

He sighed and rolled himself a smoke, feeling the sudden need for it. He drew the sweet smoke of the cigarette deep into his lungs, rubbed his chin with one hand, feeling the day's bristles hard and rough under his fingers. The last of the colour was almost gone from the sky now. Only one of the tall crests was touched with a swiftly-fading red glow. Then it, too, was gone even as he looked up at it, trying to hold it there with his eyes. The stars came out. He could see them clearly to the east, back along the way he had ridden that day. They were bright and clear there, while to the west, they had a fainter, warmer, more mellow look.

He fell to wondering if any of Sutton's men had been trailing him since he had left town. Sutton intended to get him out of his hair, there was no mistake about that and he didn't care how it was done, so long as he no longer represented a menace to the other.

Maybe the other had meant what he said and if he had seen him riding out of town he had reckoned him to be running, and would leave things like that unless he was foolish enough to ride back. He hobbled his mount after crushing out the butt of the cigarette, pulled his blankets from his saddle-roll and laid them out on the ground near the trees. Taking out his Colt, he placed it near the saddle he used as a pillow, within reach of his hand. Far off, there was the wailing cry of a coyote, followed almost at once by the eerie shrill of a quail. He listened to the night sounds crowding in on him from all sides, then drifted off into sleep.

He woke to find the stars still bright over his head, so close they might almost be touching his upturned face. He turned his head slowly, looking about him. A stone was grinding painfully into the small of his back through the thin blanket and it must have been this which had wakened him. Everything was quiet now, a deep, tangible silence that lay over the world, almost hushing his own breathing as he lay there, trying to push his gaze into the deep blackness.

He could make out the dark shape of the horse a few yards away. Nothing there to have woken him. He turned over on to his side after moving the blanket a little. It still needed four hours or so to dawn and he did not doubt that a hard day lay ahead of him, combing these desolate wastes for the man he was seeking.

He was on the point of sleep again when his horse gave a soft whinney from among the cluster of trees. It was the only sound to disturb the stillness but it brought him instantly upright, immediately wide awake. Swiftly, he reached out for the Colt, stared off into the dark, moon-thrown shadows that lay all about him. His camp was perhaps forty feet off the narrow, winding trail, half hidden from it by a clump of thick brush. Nevertheless, he could make out where the grey scar of beaten earth twisted through the coarse grass and around a couple of big, upthrusting boulders. At the moment, the trail lay empty in the flooding moonlight which made everything shine with an eerie whiteness. But that warning snicker from his mount told him there was someone – or something – close by.

Maybe a mountain cat on its nocturnal prowl, flitting silently through the shadows after its kill; perhaps only a coyote, a way off his usual hunting ground in the desert, slinking through the dimness, seeking his prey. But there was no point taking chances. Anyone trailing him from town would wait until now before trying to sneak up on him, hoping to take him off his guard.

He went forward noiselessly over the hard, springy

grass, flattened himself against one of the tall rocks, feeling it hard against his back, and waited. He did not have long to wait. His keen ears picked out the sound of an approaching rider a few minutes later. The man was coming on slow and easy. Not the way of an ordinary rider in the night, anxious to get from one place to another before the full heat of a new day, but the cautious way of a man looking for someone, knowing there might be trouble somewhere along the trail, watching the ground closely for the first sign of danger.

One of Sutton's men? The thought went through Rand's mind even as the rider came into sight, less than a hundred yards away down the trail, emerging from the black shadow between two tall boulders. It was impossible to see the other's face at that distance. The man suddenly reined his mount, bent low in the saddle, peering closely at the ground, seeking a trail. Trailing him very close, Rand thought tightly. He thinned back his lips over his teeth. The heavy .45 felt hard and reassuring in his fist. He watched as the man dismounted, began to edge forward on foot, moving along the very edge of the trail.

The man was less than twelve feet away when Rand stepped out into the middle of the trail, the Colt levelled at the other.

'Just hold it right there,' he said thinly.

The man froze but made no move towards the guns, low on his hips. He lifted his face very slowly and Rand saw, with a sudden sense of surprise, that the other had a neckerchief tied over the lower half of his face. The other's eyes watched him closely, glittering in the moonlight.

'What is this, a hold-up?' queried the other, his voice taut and hoarse, muffled by the kerchief.

Rand shook his head. 'I don't like men crowding up on me during the night, especially when they come pussy-footing it along the trail, then leave their horse back along the trail a piece and come on like you did. Seems you were lookin' for somebody in particular and I've got the feelin' it could be me.'

'You're wrong, mister,' said the other quickly, a shade too quickly. 'I never seen you before in my life.'

'Then why the mask?' Rand moved forward. 'Better take it off and let me get a good look at you.'

The man backed away a couple of paces. Rand saw his glance switch a little, until he was staring at some point over Rand's shoulder. An old trick, he thought grimly. If the other thought he was going to get out of this by trying to outsmart him, he was mistaken.

'Now do you take that mask off, or do I have to do it myself?' he grated.

'Won't do you any good,' said the other, and there was a return of confidence in his voice.

Rand made to speak, then stopped as a low voice at his back said harshly: 'Better drop that gun, mister. We don't want to have to shoot you, but we will if we have to. Our orders are to bring you in alive.'

It was Rand's turn to freeze now. He cursed himself for not having realized that there might be other men in this bunch, that the man he had seen moving along the trail had been nothing more than a decoy to attract his attention while the others sneaked up on him from behind, moving over the pine needles that lay thickly strewn over the ground, deadening the sound of their footsteps.

He saw the man in front of him move forward, hand outstretched to take the gun from him, knew that the others were close at his back. He lowered his hand to his side as if meaning to drop the Colt, then whirled swiftly, bringing it up again in a sharp sweep. Almost, he made it. But the man at his back must have been reckoning on him doing something like this, for he uttered a sharp laugh and side-stepped neatly as Rand whirled. He had been closer than Rand had thought, much closer. Even as he tried to swing the gun in his hand to cover the other, the man lifted an arm. Rand glimpsed the butt of the gun descending towards his head, saw the man's face as a pale grey blur in the dimness, heard another mocking laugh. Then something exploded with a vicious thud against the

side of his head and he pitched forward into a deep and
bottomless darkness that blotted out everything.

Coming out of the fathomless pit of unconsciousness was
a lot more painful than going into it. He was dimly aware
of a splitting agony that lanced through his brain, threatening to split his head apart. For a second, the dark
curtain lifted. He glimpsed the blinding glare of yellow
moonlight and somewhere at the back of it, several dark,
blurred shapes that stood around him, of dim faces that
stared down at him, and distant voices which spoke to him
out of the void, but which said words that he could not
understand.

Unconsciousness swept over him again and then he
dragged himself back to the surface, shook his head a
little in spite of the splitting agony of such movement
and squeezed his eyes shut, not daring to open them
until he was sure the sudden overwhelming wave of
nausea had passed from his stomach. He felt a bitter, foul
tast in his mouth and his teeth felt as though they were
covered with cottonwool. Trying to spit the taste out of
his mouth, he felt an arm at the back of his neck, lifting
his head from the ground. The cold neck of a bottle was
thrust between his teeth and the fiery liquid went down
his throat, half choking him, sending a wave of fire
through his chest.

Coughing and spluttering, he forced himself to open
his eyes. For a long moment he could see nothing for the
tears which almost blinded him. Rubbing his eyes, he sat
up. A voice close to him said thinly: 'You've only got yourself to blame for this, mister. We wanted you to come along
without any trouble. You brought it all on yourself.'

He gritted his teeth, clenching them hard until the
muscles of his jaw began to ache intolerably. He did not
understand this at all. Sutton had sworn he would kill him
if he made any trouble for him in Willard Flats and there
was no reason why he should want him alive. On the other
hand, this could have been Colter's doing. He had humil-

iated the other in front of his cronies in the saloon and the other's hatred for him would be a wild and all-consuming thing. He would want to make Rand suffer for that and a quick death was not on the cards as far as he was concerned.

'On your feet,' said the tall man he had seen on the trail. 'You're coming back with us.'

'Where are you taking me?' Rand demanded. He staggered and swayed a little as he was forced roughly to his feet.

'You'll find that out when we get there,' the other told him. He turned and motioned to one of the men who walked Rand's horse over. Under their watchful eyes, Rand climbed stiffly into the saddle, trying to think things out, but his head was aching so much, and there was a throbbing pain at the back of his eyes that he found it impossible to think clearly and he was forced to give it up. Certainly there was nothing he could do now. These men would shoot him down if he gave them any trouble. Better to string along with them until he knew what was happening.

Rand rode uneasily. He had his hands tied behind him and one of the men was leading his mount by a rope tied to the bridle. The trail wound in and out of the rocks here and he was unable to save himself whenever his mount lurched too close to one of the rough boulders. His legs were torn and bruised already and he was thankful when they finally rode down from the foothills, out on to the plain. Here, the going was easier, but the throbbing in his head continued. Any questions he directed at the men riding on either side of him were met by complete silence and in the end, he stopped asking. He tried to loosen the thongs around his wrists but they had been expertly tied and all he succeeded in doing was rubbing his flesh raw until he could feel the warmness of blood on his flesh.

It was almost dawn when they came within sight of Willard Flats. Lifting his head, Rand was able to make out the dark cluster of the buildings where they stood out on either side of the wide, main street. The men with him did not ride directly into town, but circled around, entered one of the narrow alleys that led in from the north. Rand felt a grim sense of warning. They were on the wrong side of the street for these to be Sutton's men. Yet why had they come after him with masked faces, creeping up on him during the night like that?

The man in the lead reined his mount at the side of a derelict warehouse, halfway along the alley. Smashed windows caught the first grey light of an early dawn and reflected it back dully in shards of light. But most of the place was still in shadow and the sun was nearly half an hour below the horizon yet.

'Inside,' snapped the tall man thinly. He gestured Rand down from the saddle and sat his own mount carefully, the Winchester in his hands, caught in the crook of one arm, steadying it on Rand as the other slid his leg out of the stirrup, then slipped to the ground. He almost fell, unable to help himself with his hands tied behind him, only just succeeded in keeping his balance.

Once he was down, the rest of the men alighted, moved in around him. They led him into the dark interior of the building. There was the smell of decay and dust hanging heavy in the still air and something scurried into one unlighted corner and remained poised there, red eyes glaring balefully at them as they walked by. At the far end of the building, a small group of men were seated around a long table, their faces lit by the flickering light of an oil lamp. Rand recognized three of them at once and a lot of questions were immediately answered in his mind.

'I might have figured you'd be at the back of this, Merriam,' he said harshly as he went forward. 'It had to be either you or Sutton, and I reckoned Sutton would have shot me down without botherin' to bring me back into town.'

'That's right, Kelsey,' replied the other. He swung round in his chair. 'You've got a heap of explaining to do and this time, we mean to get some answers to our questions. Before you start, I think it only fair to tell you that we're fighting for the good of the town, to protect our womenfolk from men such as Sutton and we don't care how we do it.'

'Does that include kidnapping?'

'When we're not sure of the man concerned it does,' affirmed the other tautly. He nodded to one of the men who had brought Rand in. 'Untie him, Jed. He won't try to escape.'

'You seem very sure of yourself,' Rand said, looking from one man to the other.

Merriam lifted his brows a little. 'Reckon nobody will be worrying overmuch if we were to shoot you here and now,' he said, his tone almost pleasant, as if he were discussing the weather or some business at the bank. His tone sharpened a little. 'Seems you went across the street into one of the saloons and had quite a heart-to-heart talk with Jeb Sutton yesterday afternoon shortly after leaving us. You working for him, Kelsey?'

'No. Like I told you, I'm workin' for nobody. I didn't come here to be part of this quarrel. I've seen too many towns divided like this one and I want nothing to do with it.'

'Then why talk to Sutton?' asked Foster.

'What business is that of yours?' asked Rand. He gritted his teeth as the barrel of a rifle was thrust savagely into the small of his back. Merriam waved a hand slightly and the barrel was removed.

'You don't seem to appreciate the full seriousness of your position, Kelsey. We're not fooling. We're on opposite sides of the fence to Sutton and his murdering crew, but we fight by the same rules. You ride into town with a man like Meston, start poking around, mixing with both sides and you want us to believe that you've got nothing in mind coming here.'

Rand remained silent. As yet, he was not sure how far he could trust these men. He thought of Jim Turner, the man who had come here some weeks before, the man who was, in a way, responsible for him being there; and he wondered within himself, if Tim had met up with Merriam and whether he had trusted the portly banker, only to find that this trust was misplaced, leading to his disappearance.

'You going to tell us why you're here, Kelsey?' went on the other, his voice soft, but with an undertone of menace clearly audible in it. 'Or do we have to assume that you've thrown in your lot with Sutton?'

'If you're so set against Sutton, why is it you haven't smashed him and his men for good before now?' Rand countered.

The other shrugged. 'So long as he keeps to his side of the street, we don't interfere. But there have been skirmishes at night on several occasions with men killed and wounded on both sides. Soon or later, he's going to make a try to take over the whole town and when the showdown comes, we'll be ready to fight. But we're out-numbered now and he can call on more men if he needs to. Right now, there can be only one outcome to an attack on Sutton and you can guess what that will be.'

Rand gave a brusque nod. He could guess. There had been several times in the past when the lawless element had taken over a whole town, wiping out anybody who tried to stand in their way. Certainly these Vigilantes seemed to be more organised than most others he had seen, but they were not professional killers.

'Enough of this crosstalk,' snapped Foster. 'We're getting nowhere.'

Rand glanced at him, then switched his gaze back to Merriam. The banker was still looking at him, hands flat on the table in front of him. But he seemed to have turned remote as if it were only his shell that sat there, while his spirit was miles away. Then he caught at himself, drew his mind back into the present.

'All right,' Rand said softly. 'I'll tell you why I'm here.'

'That's better,' Merriam said. 'Better be the truth though.'

'There was a man came riding into Willard Flats a few weeks ago. Jim Turner. Big man, riding a black horse.'

Merriam gave a quick nod. 'Sure, I remember him. Rode off west. Only stopped here a couple of days.'

'Any idea where he went?'

Merriam shook his head. 'Never asked. He was a man a little like you. Same sort of breed. Quiet and deep. There was some talk in the hotel that he meant to try his luck at panning for gold in the hills. But why the interest in a saddle-bum like him?'

Rand smiled thinly. 'Jim Turner was a Federal marshal. He was sent here to check on rumours of lawlessness in this part of the territory by the Governor. You sent word through asking for someone to come. Seems he must've run into big trouble.'

Merriam narrowed his eyes, then he nodded his head slowly as though in secret understanding. 'That makes sense, come to think of it,' he admitted. 'The way he would ask questions of everybody, as though he didn't mind whether you answered any of them or not; yet I reckon he got to know more of what was going on around here than anybody else.' He looked up sharply. There was a tight silence in the room. 'You figure he was killed because he found out too much?'

'That's the way I see it,' said Rand easily.

Foster said slowly. 'You a Federal marshal too, Kelsey?'

Rand shook his head. 'I'm no lawman, not officially. But Turner was a friend of mine. He saved my life during the war, risked his own doing it. I reckon I owe him something, even if it's only to find his killer and see that justice is done. That's why I came here, to find out what happened to him. He wrote me that he was headed this way, hinted at what might happen, that there could be trouble. Said he'd write again a couple of weeks later. When he didn't, I reckoned that he might have run into some kind of trouble and rode out.'

The look in Merriam's eyes told Rand that the other believed him. He said: 'If Sutton did have him followed and killed, then you'll never find his body. It could be anywhere in those hills yonder.'

'You're sure he rode out of town? Couldn't it be that he was killed here? That it was just made to look as though he'd left.'

'Could have been, but I doubt it,' said the other. 'Ain't much goes on around town that we don't know sooner or later. I saw him ride out myself. He made it pretty plain that he was going out to look for gold. From what you've told us, that was just a cover up for what he really meant to do.'

'But you've no idea what that could have been,' Rand persisted.

'Wish I had.' There was no doubting the genuineness of the other's answer. He glanced at the rest of the men, but there were only mute shakes of the head. Merriam got to his feet, scraping back his chair. He said to the man standing immediately behind Rand. 'Give him back his guns, Luke. Reckon he's all right.'

Rand took the Colts, checked the chambers, then thrust them back into the empty holsters. He felt in a sudden sombre mood now that things had come out into the open. He knew that Jim Turner had ridden into Willard Flats and that he had also ridden out again, heading west if these men were to be believed. Something must have happened to him in those hills.

'What do you intend doing now, Kelsey?' asked Merriam. He rubbed at his face, the heavy rolls of flesh quivering under his fingers.

Rand shrugged. 'Haven't made up my mind about that yet. I was in the hills hopin' to look for Turner when your boys caught up with me. I didn't have any choice about comin' back with them, I'm afraid.'

'Sorry we had to get so rough with you,' said the man called Luke. 'We were just obeying orders and for all we knew, you could have thrown in with Sutton.'

'Sure.' Rand nodded. He guessed he bore the other no ill-will. These men had been pushed to the limit of their patience by Sutton; and it was only natural they meant to take no chances. For all they knew, Sutton could have hired him in the saloon the previous day and sent him out into the hills to contact the other wild ones known to be sheltering there.

'You still going into those hills to look for Turner?' asked Merriam.

Rand smiled thinly. 'You know damned well that question doesn't need an answer,' he retorted.

'I only wanted to make sure. Some of these men will ride with you.'

'No,' Rand said, tight-lipped. 'I can handle this better alone. One man on the trail will stand a far better chance of staying hidden from anybody Sutton sends to watch those trails. By now, he may have suspected why I'm here. Even two of us would be one too many.'

'Have it your way,' said the other, tugging nervously at the straggling hairs on his upper lip. He glanced at Luke. 'Did you see anybody on the trail last night when you rode out?'

The tall man shook his head. 'Wasn't anybody there,' he affirmed. 'I figure that if Sutton is reckoning on gettin' some of those gunslingers out of the hills, he'll be waiting until he can do it without us getting wind of it.'

Outside, the cold, grey light of dawn was beginning to sift through the streets, touching the buildings with a steely light. There was no heat in the air yet, but it was soon to come. Once the sun lifted clear of the horizon, it would bring the heat with it. He moved out into the main street, eyes peeled for any sign of movement on the boardwalks. There was the sound of hammering, of metal striking metal in the distance as he rode past the mouth of one of the alleys and he guessed that the smith was up and working early.

The saloons and dance halls were silent now. A swamper appeared at the door of one of the saloons, brushing the debris of the previous night out into the street. The man paused to lift his head and stare up at the brightening sky. His gaze rested for a second on the grim-faced, tight-lipped man who rode slowly by, then he went back to his sweeping.

There was a small restaurant along the main street run by a Chinaman where breakfast was served early for the benefit of anyone wanting to get out on to the trail before the sun was really up. Rand dismounted in front of the tiny place, tethered his mount to the short rail, glanced up and down the quiet street for a moment, then pushed open the swing door and went inside.

There was no one there, even at that hour and he found himself a table near the wall where he could see both the door and the street through the window near him. Breakfast, hot and well-cooked, came within five minutes and he attacked it ravenously, hungry to the soles of his boots. At the back of the long, narrow room, Ah Fong worked over the ancient stove, his back to Rand. He wore a dark pigtail down the centre of his back, a faded pair of blue jeans and a yellow work shirt. Rand studied the man thoughtfully, decided that he might know something. Turning, he caught Rand's eye, came over with an earthenware jug of black coffee.

'You like some more, cowboy?' he asked.

Rand nodded, sat back in his chair as the other poured his coffee. Sipping it, Rand said quietly: 'Seems pretty slack today. Don't you usually get more than this in so early?'

'Usually many come, but not today,' said the other enigmatically.

Rand glanced at him in surprise. 'Why? Something special about today?'

The other nodded his head wisely, dark eyes gleaming a little, the faint air of mystery about him, his tone lowered a little as if he were imparting some information of tremendous importance.

'Most of the men have gone to one of their meetings. The Vigilantes.'

'Sure, I see.' Rand drank the coffee black, ignoring the cream and sugar which the other had set down before him. 'The Vigilantes. I've heard a lot of them. Seems to me they're wasting their time. Sutton will beat them if they try to stop him. Even with the men he's got he could do it, but if he decides to call in those *hombres* from the hills, nothing could stop him.'

'Perhaps,' nodded the other wisely. 'But Mister Merriam has sent word to the Governor warning him of the situation here in Willard Flats. Soon we will get help.'

'I heard about that. Seems it's a long time for him to be hearing from the Governor. They tell me he asked for that help some months ago. I'd have thought there would have been somebody here before now.'

The other eyed him with an oriental, inscrutable stare for a long moment, then poured out another cup of coffee. His movement was half-shrug, half-shudder. 'Could be that somebody did come,' he said quietly. 'But maybe Mister Sutton got to hear of it first and took steps to see that he did not cause trouble for him.'

'What sort of steps?' Rand tried to keep too much curiosity out of his voice.

'In China we have saying. Man who watch fly all the time, see spider too.'

Rand smiled. 'Now what is that supposed to mean?'

'Quite simple. Sutton had somebody watching for any stranger riding into this territory. Could be this man made friends with Mister Turner, became a man he thought he could trust. That way, it would be easy for Sutton to know everything that was being done, plan everything down to last detail.'

Rand nodded. 'Ah Fong,' he said quietly. 'You are a very wise man.'

'Thank you.' The Chinaman moved away from the table, then paused. 'You want more coffee?'

Rand shook his head. 'An excellent meal,' he said. 'But tell me. Did you know this man Turner at all?'

'He used to come here to eat. Quiet man, sat in the

corner there every time, watching the door. He was a man used to trouble, I could tell that, always on the alert for it. Then he rode out one morning, never came back.'

'Merriam seems to think he went out looking for gold. If that's the case, then there's no reason to suppose he'll be back in town for some months yet, until he needs further supplies.'

Ah Fong shook his head emphatically. 'He did not ride out for gold. I know that.'

'How could you possibly know? Did he tell you where he was going – and why?'

'Not exactly where, but he told me why he was going.'

'Did he now?' Rand stared at the other in momentary surprise. It was not all that difficult to believe, he told himself. A man like Ah Fong would be the last person to betray a man to Jeb Sutton and it was just possible that Jim Turner had had a premonition that he might be riding into far bigger trouble than he could hope to handle. He might have left word with someone. Why not with this Chinaman who looked as innocent as an unspanked babe?

'Were you a friend of Jim Turner's?' There was a look of gathering awareness in the other's eyes now and his lips were drawn back a little, showing the gold-filled teeth.

'I owe him my life,' said Rand simply. 'I knew he was headed this way and I rode out to try to meet up with him. Seems I missed him by a few weeks.'

'He said that a man might come looking for him, asking questions about him. A man like you.'

'Did he tell you anything to tell me?' asked Rand eagerly.

Ah Fong nodded his head slowly. He opened his mouth to speak, then paused, lifted his head quickly as the tiny bell above the street door tinkled and someone came in. Rand glanced round, saw Meston slide into the room. The other spotted him at once, lifted a heavy hand in greeting.

'I'll see you in the alley in twenty minutes,' hissed Ah Fong in Rand's ear. Bobbing his head, he moved off towards Meston. The other advanced on Rand and motioned to the empty chair opposite him. 'Mind if I join you, Kelsey?' he asked.

Rand shook his head. 'Help yourself,' he said. He threw a quick look in Ah Fong's direction, but the other had his back to him, was bending over the hot stove at the far end of the room. He looked back to Meston. The other was eyeing him curiously with a strange glint in his close-set eyes.

Rand said: 'Aren't you scared a little, walking around town like this? What will happen if Sutton decides to finish what he started a while ago?'

The other smiled viciously. ' I figure that so long as I stay on this side of the street he won't bother with me,' he answered. 'I'm small fry as far as he's concerned. He's much more interested in a certain other person.'

'Meanin' me?' said Rand directly.

'That's it.'

Rand remained silent. He was turning over in his mind what Ah Fong had said. Did the other really know something important? Could he give him the lead he really needed now? If he could, it would enable him to track down Jim Turner wherever he might be. Already, the trail would have grown cold and he needed help of some kind.

'I thought I saw you head out of town yesterday,' Meston was saying, not looking up. 'I figured you'd have taken the hint and ridden out while you had the chance, yet I see you're back in town again. What happened? Did you change your mind about Sutton, or was it changed for you?'

'Like I told Sutton, I might like it here and if I did, then I intended to stay. Nobody has scared me off yet and it's too late to start now.'

'If I were you, I wouldn't buck Sutton too much. He may not look a hard *hombre*, but believe me, there's a snake's mind at the back of that face. He'd as soon shoot you dead as he would a rattler and with just as little thought about it. He doesn't have a conscience.'

'I've handled rattlers before,' Rand said harshly. Ah

Fong brought Meston's breakfast and set it down in front of him. For just the barest fraction of a second, his gaze strayed in Rand's direction, then he had turned on his heel and moved away, his slippers making soft shuffling sounds on the floor.

Rand waited, sitting back in his chair, outwardly calm and relaxed, but his mind was far from calm. Meston ate rapidly, pushed the empty plate away from him, drank the coffee in quick, noisy gulps. When he was finished, he said meaningly: 'If you want my advice, you'll leave town right away. This whole place is goin' to blow up in our faces at any moment. If you decide to stay here and make it your quarrel, no matter which side you back, you'll only get yourself hurt.'

Thrusting back his chair, he got heavily to his feet, looked down at Rand for a long moment, then touched the scars around his neck with his fingertips. 'I know what I'm talking about,' he said ominously.

When he had gone, Rand looked round for Ah Fong, but while he had been talking to Meston, the other had slipped away into the back of the restaurant. Shrugging, he got to his feet, went outside, stood for a moment on the sidewalk, looking up and down the street. Willard Flats was coming to life now. To the west, far in the distance, he could make out the tall, sky-rearing peaks of the hills, now tipped with a rosy flush as the sun just lifted clear of the eastern horizon. A gust of air sighed along the dusty street, bowling a few balls of dry brush in front of it, sending them rustling eerily along the edge of the boardwalk.

He lit a cigarette, smoked it slowly, savouring it, It brought a calmness to his frayed nerves. Things were happening a little too fast for his liking now, building up to an early showdown. Not that he doubted his ability to cope with the problem, but he liked to know just what was stacked against him and he had the feeling that things were happening about which he knew nothing; and he didn't like that in the least.

Waiting until he had finished his smoke, he dropped

the butt on to the ground and crushed it under his heel. Nobody seemed to be paying him any real attention at the moment and he walked slowly and casually along the road, then turned into the narrow alley that ran between two tall buildings. He flicked his gaze over it as he made his way forward, still alert for trouble, but it seemed empty and there was no sound in that direction.

Ah Fong had said he would be waiting for him at the other end. Halfway along the alley, he paused, sensing some kind of danger, yet not sure from which direction it would come. Not a sound disturbed the clinging stillness. Quiet, too quiet.

He went on again, clambered over a pile of bricks and debris which littered the alley, stretching from one side to the other. Ah Fong must have gone through the back of the restaurant, he reflected, cursing a little as he half fell on the rubbish. Certainly no one had come this way for some time, otherwise the rubble would have been disturbed.

Reaching the end of the alley, he looked about him cautiously. There was no sign of the Chinese restaurant owner there and he felt a little nagging sense of worry in his mind. Had something happened to the other? Or was it just that more clients had turned up and he had been forced to serve them before being able to slip away to meet him?

Easing his way forward, he turned into the narrower alley that led off from the other, back in the direction of the rear of the restaurant. A moment later, he saw the legs in the faded blue jeans sticking out from behind a pile of cans. Ab Fong lay face downward in the dirt and dust, head twisted a little, eyes open and staring sightlessly at the blue sky. There was still that strangely inscrutable look on his face even in death, and the hilt of a knife sticking from between his shoulders, a red stain of blood soaking into the yellow shirt.

FIVE

ACCUSATION!

Slowly, Rand went down on one knee beside the other. One look had been enough to tell him that there was nothing he or anyone else could do for the little Chinaman. The other's body was still warm and he guessed that he had been killed only a few moments before, perhaps while he had been standing out front, in the main street, smoking that cigarette. If he had come straight here he might have been able to prevent this. He felt the hardness grow in him again. Now he knew for certain that Ah Fong had known something important about Jim Turner and he had been killed to prevent him from talking.

Slowly, he got to his feet, rubbed his chin for a moment, then stopped abruptly as a harsh voice behind him grated: 'Lift your hands, Kelsey, where I can see 'em.'

He hesitated for a moment, then raised his hands slowly, turning as he did so. Sheriff Blane stood a few yards away, the heavy Colt in his hand trained on Rand's chest. His finger was tight on the trigger and his unwavering glance never left the other's face. There were a couple more men behind him, men that Rand did not recognize.

'Now see here, Sheriff,' Rand said quickly. 'If you figure I did this, then you're wrong. I arranged to meet Ah Fong here a little while ago. He was dead when I got here.'

'So you say,' drawled the other. He stepped forward. 'Shuck that gunbelt, then move ahead of me to the jail-house.'

'You've got no right arrestin' me for this,' Rand said through his teeth. 'You got no proof at all.'

Blane's grin widened a shade. He motioned to the two men behind him. 'You do as I say, Kelsey, or these men will be witness that I shot you for resistin' the law.'

So that was the way it was, Rand thought tightly. If there had ever been a frame against him, this was it. These three men had arrived on the scene a little too quickly for it to be sheer coincidence. Either they had been waiting for him to arrive, or they had been tipped off by the man who had actually done the killing. Either way, it did not look as if he would have much of a chance to beat this rap. He doubted if Merriam and the other citizens of the Vigilante Committee would be able to help him, even if they wished to do so. Things certainly looked black against him.

Reluctantly, he unbuckled the gunbelt and let it drop into the dust. Blane relaxed visibly. 'Now you're being sensible,' he said softly. 'We don't want any more trouble here. Ah Fong was a respected citizen of Willard Flats. A lot of folk liked him and they won't have any sympathy with his killer.'

Rand said through his teeth. 'Like I said, this has been rigged against me. That isn't my knife in his back and you won't be able to prove it is.'

Blane raised the thick, bushy brows a little. He seemed to be enjoying himself. 'I don't have to prove that, Kelsey. It's up to you to prove to a jury that it ain't yours, and you might find that difficult to do. We found you here stand-ing over the body and I reckon Doc Stone will be able to testify that he hasn't been dead more'n a few minutes. Could be there'll be plenty of other witnesses to say he was in the restaurant only a little while ago. And we know you were there ten minutes ago, having a meal.'

'Why should I want to kill him? I didn't even know him.'

'Do you jaspers need to know every man you kill?' Blane stepped forward, motioning with his gun. 'Move along to the jailhouse and don't make any funny moves or I'll use this.'

Rand walked to the jail with the three men moving close at his back. In the street, he noticed the curious stares he got from the folk on both sides of the road. As they neared the sheriff's office, Merriam came hurrying up. He called harshly. 'What's happenin' here, Sheriff? Why is this man under arrest?'

'I've arrested him on a charge of murder, Mister Merriam,' said the other tightly.

'Murder?' There was a blank look on the banker's face. 'I don't believe it. If he shot a man, it would be in fair fight and that isn't murder.'

'He didn't shoot him,' Blane said thickly. 'He used a knife on Ah Fong. His body is back in the alley yonder. We found this *hombre* bending over him when we got there.'

'And who tipped you off that he'd been murdered?' asked Rand loudly, as they stopped just outside the office. He turned to face Blane, saw the sudden look of uncertainty on the man's flabby features, knew that this was something that the sheriff could not answer without incriminating himself. 'You said yourself he'd been dead only a minute or so by the time you got there. What were you doing in the alley? Could be that you killed him because he knew too much about Jim Turner.'

Blane's face blanched at the other's name but he struggled to keep some of his dignity. He said blusteringly, 'I'm not on trial, Kelsey. You're the one who is goin' to have to answer these questions and in front of a jury at that.'

He moved forward, thrusting the barrel of his gun into Rand's ribs. 'Get inside and we'll have no more talking until the circuit judge gets here in a couple of days. Then we'll show you how swift justice can be here on the frontier.'

'Just a minute, Blane,' snapped Merriam. 'There's somethin' here that doesn't sound right to me. I saw

Kelsey myself not five minutes ago, standing yonder, outside the restaurant smoking a cigarette. You say he went along the alley and murdered Ah Fong by putting a knife in his back.'

'That's the way it looked to me,' muttered Blane. He glared around at the banker. 'Better stay out of this, Merriam, unless you want to get involved in it as well. This *hombre* ain't worth it. I'm tellin' you, I know his kind. They ride into a strange town, pick a quarrel with one of the citizens and before we know it, somebody is dead, either in a gunfight in the main street, or with a knife in their back in some alley.'

Merriam shook his head. 'You can't arrest a man on flimsy evidence like that, Blane, and it seems to me that you ain't got no evidence at all, except that Kelsey happened to be there when you arrived on the scene. Come to think of it, how did you happen along so conveniently?' The banker's eyes bored into the lawman's.

Blane swallowed thickly, turned appealingly to the two men who had backed him up, but Rand noticed that they seemed to be more interested in something going on at the far end of the street, than in trying to find a plausible answer to that particular question. Finally, Blane said tartly: 'Well, maybe we was a mite hasty accusin' you, Kelsey, but you got to admit that things did look bad against you when we found you in that alley.' His eyes narrowed just a shade and Rand knew that he was fighting down a deep-seated wrath at the way in which the banker had interfered in this deal. Rand had no illusions. If he had not put his cards on the table in front of that Vigilante Committee earlier that morning, he would have been safely locked away in the jail and there might even be a lynching mob getting set for some quick justice before high noon.

'You settin' me free, Sheriff?' he asked quietly. 'If so, I'd like my guns back.'

The veins were standing out like cords in the lawman's neck. For a moment, it seemed he was on the point of ignoring commonsense, that he would even shoot Rand down there and then and attempt to justify his action later. Then he swallowed thickly, nodded to one of the men at his back. 'Hand him back his guns, Chuck,' he said thinly. His gaze swept over Rand and there was both anger and warning in it. 'I still reckon you killed him, Kelsey, though I ain't got no real proof of it, not enough to hold you on suspicion anyway. But I'll be keepin' my eyes and ears open, and the minute I hear anythin' against you, I'll come ridin' after you.'

'That's a fair warning, I reckon,' Rand said, holstering his guns. He gave a brief shrug of his shoulders.

'Take it that way,' said the other through his teeth. Turning, he stumped angrily into the office, slamming the door behind him.

Merriam came up to Rand and said softly: 'Is it true about Ah Fong? That he's been murdered?'

'I'm afraid it is. I know why he was murdered too. He mentioned in the restaurant that Jim Turner had given him some information on why he was ridin' up into the hills. Ah Fong was goin' to tell me what it was when Meston came in and he promised to meet me at the end of the alley ten minutes later. When I got there someone had been there before me and he was dead.'

'I see.' Merriam's lips tightened. 'Seems that someone doesn't want you to find out what happened to your friend. What can you do now, the trail will be cold?'

'I'm goin' to ride out there anyway and snoop around. I might find something to give me a lead. I've got a feeling that whoever killed Ah Fong was certain that I'd be arrested for his murder. Either they tipped off the sheriff, or it was one of those two *hombres* with him. They may get a little over-confident and if that happens, they'll make a mistake sooner or later and I mean to be around when that happens.'

He knew he had a job in hand as he rode along the narrow valley that lifted ten miles further on and branched out into the myriad trails which led up into the hills. The thing had not formed exactly in his mind yet, what he was really going to do once he reached the hills and had to start looking for a clue to Turner's whereabouts. He did what he had always done whenever he had a problem that needed sorting; he had ridden straight at it, hoping that if he let things take their natural course, something was sure to break sooner or later. On this occasion, however, he had the unshakeable feeling that time was one commodity he had very little of.

He gave his mount its head while they were on the flat, making good time, knowing that once he hit the rising ground, he would be forced to slow. Even though he doubted if he would be trailed again, he continued to check his back-trail, keeping a watchful eye on the ground to either side of him. It was not unknown for a bush-whacker to ride parallel with the man he meant to try to kill. But he saw nothing in the higher country to either side of the valley.

Came high noon and he was halfway along the valley. A stream crossed the trail and he slid from the saddle when he reached it, let the horse drink its fill, glad of the way it thrust its muzzle right under the water as it drank, the sign of a real thoroughbred animal. In the heat, with the hills shimmering as if behind a curtain of water, there was a deep and pendant stillness over everything. It was as if a curtain of silence had been dropped over the entire area, shutting off all sounds. Not a bird cheeped in the brush and there was not even the lowing of any cattle in the vicinity although the grass here was of the best. Strange that no one had thought to come out here and take this land, he reflected as he stood on top of a low rise, and looked about him. A man could build up a fine herd of cattle here and the land seemed good for more than just beef. It would grow good crops too.

There had been times when he had hoped to be able to find a place like this with the tall hills marching grandly along the horizons, with a warm sun and a stream running right down through the middle of it; but for a while now, with the restlessness brought on in him by the war, he had pushed such thoughts right into the back of his mind, seldom bringing them out into the open for an airing.

He rode through the long afternoon, not stopping once, and evening found him once more high in the hills. Clouds were building up to the west and he knew he would be forced to sleep wet that night. Making camp, he pulled his blankets beneath the overhanging branches of a couple of tall trees where there would be some shelter from the rain when it came. He ate supper cold, not risking a fire. By the time he was rolled in his blankets, the few stars which had been visible a little while before were all but swamped by the scudding clouds and heavy raindrops began to fall. He pulled the blanket more tightly about his neck and fell asleep.

Dawn still brought the rain, drifting in sheets down the hillside as he rolled out of his blanket and got to his feet. There was a coolness in the air and things looked dismal and grey, lacking the colour brought to them by the sun. He rolled up his blanket, hitched it on to the saddle, let the horse graze for a while, as he smoked. He felt a continuing worry in his mind, but he tried not to think about it. Jim Turner was up here someplace. He felt sure of that. If he could only find him. Dead or alive, if he once found him, he would know where he stood and what he had to do.

Mounting up, he rode slowly forward, moving upgrade where the trail played out through rock and gravel. Wind touched his face, its coldness beginning to soak into him, yet when he took off his hat to rub his forehead, sweat dripped into his eyes. Soon, it mingled with the rain that beat against him, driven at him by the wind, and he lowered his head a little as he rode into the storm. There was only the consolation that if anyone was trailing him, they would be forced to undergo the same discomforts as he was.

He rose higher with short, switchback courses that

lifted him up the side of the hill. Here and there, he saw
evidence of works beside small creeks that flowed swiftly
downhill. Men had been here, he thought, panning the
streams for the precious yellow metal with which they
hoped to bring themselves a fortune. Yet even when they
did make a strike, they would lose it all in town, cheated
out of it by the cardsharps and sharks in the saloons,
rubbed of what little they had left when they finally staggered out into the street. A fool and his gold . . . Rand
thought.

A new slide of earth blocked the trail in front of him as
he rounded a sharply-angled bend in the trail. He reined
his mount and sat looking at it for a long moment. On one
side, the trail dropped away for a sheer two hundred feet
on to the jagged rocks below. On the other, the rocky wall
lifted for another twenty feet or more; and there was less
than two feet on the precipice side of the slide for a rider
to ease past.

Deciding against riding the horse along that danger-
ously narrow part of the trail, he slid from the saddle,
caught lightly at the bridle, and led the animal forward,
coaxing it on. It dug in its forelegs as it reached the edge
of the slide, whinneyed softly as it resisted his pull. He
spoke softly and gently to it and slowly, it moved forward,
placing one foot gingerly in front of the other while Rand
wormed his way backward past the slide on to the firmer
ground of the trail at the other side. Inch by inch, the
horse came forward. Had it not been a thoroughbred, he
doubted if it would have obeyed or trusted him. As it was,
they only just made it with scant inches to spare.

By mid-morning, he was on the edge of a small mountain lake. Long, bright shafts of sunlight fingered through
the tall pines which bordered it. The skies had cleared
while he had been climbing steadily and now there were
broad gaps in them through which the blue was showing.

A sharp breeze, blowing off the crests of the peaks
which surrounded the lake, rippled the surface and sent
white waves dancing across it. During the ride through the

pines, he had spotted a couple of wooden shacks just above the timberline and he skirted the lake, making for them. They showed at intervals through gaps in the thick trees and it was not until he encountered the small stage at the water's edge, made out of rough-hewn planks and the trail which wound up into the trees in the direction of the cabins that he felt any stirring of excitement in his mind.

Men had been here at some time in the recent past, he guessed, might still be there. They might conceivably be some of the wild ones he knew to be sheltering here, men who lived by the gun, cruel and vicious as some of the animals who hunted here; men who would throw in with Sutton and help him take over the town and surrounding territory if it came to a showdown with the Vigilantes.

He rode slowly along the rising trail, came out into a clearing. The two shacks faced him, set against a wall of smooth rock. Even from that distance, it was obvious they were deserted. An axe had been thrust into a tree trunk, the haft sticking out at a sharp angle, the head rusted a little now. A man had swung it into the wood, the head biting deep, and then he had simply walked away and left it there, never to come back. Such were the ways of life out here in the hills and mountains, Rand mused. Men came to work their lives away, seeking both solitude and a fortune in gold. Either they found it or they left, sadder and wiser men. But in the end, they all left, and the mountains and forests remained as they had been for countless ages before, timeless and aloof. The wind soughed through the bending boughs of the pine trees as he moved steadily out towards the shacks. There was a feel about this place that he did not like, something he couldn't put his finger on and say it was anything definite, but it was there. A little spot between his shoulder blades began to itch as if someone were standing in the shadows of the tall trees, drawing a bead on him with a rifle at that very moment.

With an effort, he shook off the feeling, telling himself

that he was imagining it all. There was no one within miles of this place. To his left, there was nothing but the long sweep of the valley which had the lake at its end, all rises and slopes, with the pines standing like a green carpet on the lowermost slopes. Above them, the gaunt bare rock lifted sheer to the blue heavens. Everything looked peaceful, he mused. He stepped down from his mount at the entrance to the nearer of the two cabins, moved cautiously forward.

Inside, in the gloomy interior, he found everything as its owner had left it some years before. There was a thin layer of grey dust on the floor and covering the table. Nothing had disturbed the dust and this told him, more plainly than anything else, that no one had been here, not even seeking shelter from the winter storms which could come sweeping down without warning.

He hunted around, found nothing of interest, and moved towards the other shack. Pausing in the doorway, he peered inside. On the face of it, everything seemed the same as he had noticed in the other building. Then his eyes narrowed slightly as he noticed the marks on the long table in the centre of the shack. Going forward, he examined them carefully. They had not been caused by rats, he reasoned. Someone had been here very recently. A fire had been lit in the stove, and bending his nostrils caught the sharp odour of burnt wood. Going back outside, he began to hunt around, obsessed now with the feeling that something had happened here, not many weeks before.

Five minutes later, he found what he had been looking for. The body had been dragged into a clump of thorn bushes growing out of the thin, dry soil at the base of the rocks. Gently, he turned the other over, felt his blood freeze momentarily in his veins. He knew now how Jim Turner had died. Three bullet holes in his back told Rand that whoever had shot him down, probably from ambush, had not meant that he should live to testify to his attacker's identity.

Kneeling beside the dead man, his mind dulled and

empty by what he had found, Rand went systematically through the dead marshal's pockets. There were the usual items there, and in the vest pocket, he found the metal star, blood-stained but still bright. Acting on impulse, he slipped it into his own pocket, not sure why he did it.

Returning to one of the shacks, he moseyed around until he turned up a shovel, carried it outside and began to dig. Once he had cut through the thin topsoil, the going was hard. He struck rock less than two feet down and the spade refused to bite through it. Unwilling to give up, he found a pick and used it to continue his digging. It was hard and tiring work, and he was forced to halt on several occasions. The sun burned through the few remaining clouds and his body was soaked in sweat long before he had finished digging the grave to his liking. He ate a hurried meal while the sun was at its zenith, carried on with his chore during the early part of the afternoon. When he was finished, he tossed the pick and shovel out of the hole, pulled himself out with a wrench of arm and shoulder muscles. It was then that he heard the steady abrasion of an approaching horse, heading up the trail from the direction of the lake. As yet, he could not see the rider for the trees and, bending low, he ran back in the direction of the shack nearby, grabbing at his rifle as he did so.

The rider halted among the trees, seemed to be deliberating whether to advance further into the clearing. Evidently the other had already spotted the horse tethered in front of the shacks. Carefully, Rand lifted the rifle, heard a voice mutter something to the horse, then the rider came into view, emerging from the trees and he lowered the weapon in sudden surprise. The sunlight, slanting into the clearing, glistened on the golden hair under the wide-brimmed black hat perched on the back of the girl's head. She sat her mount easily, evidently accustomed to the saddle, looking about her in perplexity.

Moving out into the open, Rand lowered the rifle, saw

A Day to Die

the instant stiffening of the girl's body, the way her right hand moved quickly to the rifle in the scabbard.

'Who are you?' she asked tightly. 'What are you doing here?'

'I might ask you the same question,' Rand said, speaking evenly.

She jerked her head a little, as if unaccustomed to being spoken to like this, then said sharply. 'I was down by the lake when I heard someone up here. This place has been empty and deserted for more than ten years. Nobody comes here any more.'

'I'm afraid someone has been here more recently than that,' Rand said slowly. He nodded his head towards Turner's body near the other building. 'I was getting set to bury him when I heard you coming along. Sorry about the rifle, but I had heard that there are men around these parts who would shoot first and ask questions later. Better to be a mite inhospitable than dead, I always say.'

'Who is it?' There was a faint quaver in the girl's tone as she slid from the saddle and moved toward a little. She was no longer quite so sure of herself.

'His name was Jim Turner,' Rand said slowly. 'He was a friend of mine. I've been looking for him for some weeks now. I didn't expect to find him like this.'

'Has he been shot?'

'Shot in the back three times,' Rand said grimly. 'I guess whoever did it, wanted to make sure he wouldn't survive and talk.'

'These hills are full of outlaws,' the girl said throatily. She looked about her as she spoke, as if expecting to see someone close by at that very moment.

'How come they don't worry you?'

'We have a small spread on the other side of the lake. My name's Lois Venning. It's only a small place and so long as we don't interfere with the hill folk, they don't bother us. It's an uneasy arrangement, but it seems to work.'

'Rand Kelsey,' said Rand, introducing himself. He wiped his brow with the back of his hand.

'Have you ridden here from Willard Flats?'

He nodded. 'Left there yesterday. A Chinese restaurant owner told me that Jim here had headed out of town into the hills. I was taking any trail I found, hoping I might find him. Spotted these shacks earlier this morning from down by the lake and came up, hoping I might find someone who could give me some information. Instead, I found Jim's body, hidden in those bushes yonder.'

'It would be Ah Fong who had told you about your friend.'

'He told me a little.' Rand's tone was suddenly grim and the girl glanced at him in mild surprise. 'But he couldn't tell me everything he knew. Somebody got to him before that and killed him, knifed him in the back.'

The girl put a hand to her throat, stared at him with widening eyes. 'Ah Fong – murdered?'

'I'm afraid so, Miss Venning. Seemed that somebody didn't want me to find Jim Turner.'

'Now that you have, what do you intend to do?'

'Once I've buried him, I'm headin' back into town to try to find his killer and when I do, justice will be quick and sure.' There was no bravado in his tone as he made this threat, only a quiet sureness of intent, and the girl had the unshakeable feeling that what this man swore he would do, would be done in spite of everything.

Carefully, he lowered Turner's body into the grave, stood at the end for a moment holding his hat in his hands, then glanced a little helplessly at the girl standing beside him. 'It doesn't seem right to let him go like this, without saying something over him,' he said finally. 'Trouble is I never was one for religion and I don't know anything.'

She nodded her head slowly. 'I never knew him,' she said, 'but I think he was a good man.' Rand threw a handful of dirt into the hole and then stood quite still while the girl said softly: 'Man that is born of woman hath but a short while to live and is full of misery . . .'

Suddenly, everything seemed more hushed and still than before and Rand knew some of the loneliness that must have been in Jim Turner when he had ridden up here seeking trouble, and finding it.

'. . . though I walk through the Valley of the Shadow of Death I will fear no evil, for Thou art with me. Thy rod and Thy staff shall comfort me . . .'

Strange, he thought inwardly, that their trails should meet again like this, should meet only to be torn apart. He felt a moment of sadness, and close on its heels came a deep and surging anger that bit right through him so that in spite of himself, he clenched his hands tightly by his sides, the nails digging painfully into the flesh of the palms.

'. . . Thou preparest a table before me in the presence of mine enemies and I will dwell in the house of the Lord forever.'

He looked up quickly, saw that the girl had fallen silent, almost expectantly.

'Amen,' he said abruptly. Without another word he bent, picked up the flat shovel and began to fill in the deep hole, covering up the body of the man who had been Jim Turner, Federal marshal.

They rode slowly out of the wide clearing, down the winding trail which led to the calm, placid waters of the lake, gleaming bluely now in the sunlight of the late afternoon. There was not a cloud to be seen in the sky and everywhere lay the sharp smell of the pines and the utter stillness that a man could find only in the high mountains and open places.

'Won't you ride on with me to the ranch?' asked Lois Venning as they reached the water's edge. 'It's only a little way around the lake and it will save you having to camp out in the open tonight. You'll never make it back to town before dark.'

'Why thank you.' Rand nodded gratefully. He had not been looking forward to sleeping out on the trail, especially when he did not really dare to light a fire, and although he was used to eating cold, he did not want to refuse the offer of well-cooked food.

The girl wheeled her mount, rode out on to a broader trail than that which had led them down the hillside. The girl had started cool and suspicious of him and for a while, she had evidently wanted to keep it that way. But now that she knew a little of what had been riding him and why he had been there, there seemed to be a lot more warmth in her than he had at first thought. The road reached through a narrow canyon, still on the level, then moved downgrade for a piece before levelling out once more as they swung around the northern edge of the wide lake. Rand noticed that it widened here at this end and guessed that the Venning ranch would get most of its water from here. It was good country and he wondered how this family managed to live on such peaceful terms with the wild ones. Maybe, as the girl herself had told him, it was a situation of mutual agreement. Neither side interfered with the other. A plank bridge led over a small stream which fed into the lake, the water running swiftly over the rocky bottom, bubbling into white-plumed foam here and there whenever one of the larger rocks split the surface.

In another three minutes, they were at the front of a log house, built long and low across the yard. Beyond it, where the ground opened out into a long meadow, he saw a small herd of cattle grazing peacefully in the lush grass and there was a small barn near the house with a couple of horses just visible in the dim-lit interior.

A man came out into the doorway, stood watching them with a faintly curious expression on his face. Sliding from the saddle, the girl called out: 'I met this man up at the old mine, Dad. I offered him a meal and bed for the night.'

The other gave a quick nod, smiled a faint greeting. 'Strangers are welcome here,' he said. For a moment, he seemed neither interested nor disinterested in Rand. Then he nodded towards the barn. 'You can put your mount up there. See he gets a cup of coffee, Lois.'

The girl led the way to the barn, waited until he had attended to his mount, then went back to the house with him, led him through a narrow passageway and into the kitchen. Setting a pot of coffee on the edge of the stove, she motioned him to a chair at the table.

'Do you run this place by yourselves?' Rand asked. 'Seems a lot to do without any men around.'

'We manage,' said the girl softly. 'Since mother died, five years ago, we've had to do things as best we could. Fortunately the weather here is usually good. Back east, before we came out here, things were made more difficult by the droughts we had, when most of the cattle would die for want of water. We don't have that trouble here. Sometimes we get a violent storm during the winter, but that's all, and as I said, we have little trouble from the outlaws in the hills.'

She took down a cup from a hook on the wall, placed it in front of him, took the coffee from the stove and poured it for him, pointing to the milk and the sugar box. She poured a drink for herself, then sat down in the chair opposite him and watched him curiously. She was still a little puzzled and uncertain about him. 'Do you think you'll find the man who shot your friend?'

Rand gave a cynical grin. 'I know who gave the order to have him killed.'

He saw the sudden look on her face, gave a brief nod. 'I reckon you know who it was too. If you've ever ridden into Willard Flats lately, you're bound to know.'.

'Jeb Sutton?' It was more of a statement than a question.

'Nobody else.' Rand made to say something more but at that moment the kitchen door opened and the tall man came in. Venning said: 'Lois mentioned you were up at the old mine. You looking for gold?'

Rand shook his head. 'I was looking for a friend of

mine who was supposed to have ridden into the hills six weeks ago.'

'Did you find him?' Something on the girl's face seemed to stop the man and his brows lifted a little as he turned to look in Rand's direction.

'I found him.' Hardness touched Rand's voice. His grip on the cup in his hand tightened convulsively. 'He'd been shot three times in the back. His guns were still in their holsters. He never had a chance to defend himself.'

'I see.' The other nodded. 'And now you'll be riding the vengeance trail as soon as you leave here. That's what usually happens.'

'You figure I ought to forget all about it? Treat it as if nothing had happened?'

The other spread his hands wide. 'I once thought as you did,' he said quietly, seriously. 'I only had one real friend and they hung him for something he didn't do. I wanted to get every man on that jury, even the men in the hanging team, and shoot down each one of them. That was my personal feud. But one soon gets to realize that this solves nothing. You go on killing and there's eventually only one possible end to it.'

'I like to see a man get an even chance,' said Rand tightly.

Venning gave him an over-bright glance. 'There are ways out here which you cannot even begin to understand. Do you think I would be alive today, that I would still have this small homestead if I'd decided that the outlaws who infest this territory ought to be brought to justice and I decided to set myself up against them. Live and let live is my motto now. It's stood me in good stead since I came here. I'm tolerated by them and so long as I don't step out of line, try to line myself up with Merriam and the Vigilante Committee they've started in town, they leave me alone.'

'Trouble is, that if everybody did that, they'd step in and take over the whole country. You're tolerated only because they consider that you're too small to be noticed.

If there was no Vigilante Committee to bother them, they would soon start looking round and they'd pick on you. You have to keep law and order, and with men like this, the only way to do it is to fight. That's what my friend was doing here.'

There was a faint spark of interest in Venning's eyes as he glanced at Rand across the table. 'Your friend was a lawman?'

'That's right. Seems Merriam wrote to the Governor asking for help against Sutton and his crew. Turner was sent here to check on what was happening. It seems he trusted someone too much and they decided to get rid of him the only way they knew.'

'And now you're all fired-up to avenge his death.'

'He saved my life, during the war. If it hadn't been for him I would have been killed, left to bleed to death under the enemy's guns. He carried me clear, risking his life to do so. I figure this is the least I can do for him.'

'So be it,' nodded the other. 'I won't try to turn a man from his chosen path, whether I agree with it or not. But this could be the road to perdition for you, I suppose you realize that.'

'I know it's the only trail I can follow,' Rand said carefully. He knew that the girl was watching him closely as he spoke. 'A man can never go back and ride the same trail twice, but he can always turn from one to another and hope that he's swinging back to the one he ought to follow.'

Rand ate breakfast in the dining-room the next morning. When he had finished, he moved at once into the thin and winey air outside. There was still a coolness there and he stood quite still, drawing the sweet-smelling air down into his lungs. The morning had that freshness to it which made it good to be alive. There was a soft step behind him and the girl came out on to the porch. She stood with one arm upraised, fingers resting lightly on the wooden upright. There was a strange quality in her voice as she said: 'You really intend to ride back into town and hunt out your friend's killer?'

'I've got to,' he said thinly, speaking through his teeth. 'Not only Jim's killer, but also the man who murdered Ah Fong because he knew too much, the man who wants to hold all of this territory to ransom.'

'Sutton.'

'And his men, in particular that foreman of his – Colter.'

'I've heard that he's a killer, that Sutton brought him here from Texas to back up any play he wanted to make.'

'That I can believe.' Rand curled a cigarette in his fingers, put the tobacco pouch back into his pocket, lit the cigarette and drew the smoke down into his lungs. His thoughts were running fast and uncertain in his mind, too fast for his liking. If Colter decided to run, it might mean a long and weary search for him, perhaps as long and as weary as that which had just finished for him now that he had at last found Jim Turner.

He brought his horse out of the barn, threw the saddle on him, tightened the cinch under the animal's belly, checked the rifle in its scabbard, then swung up easily.

'I wish you would reconsider and stay here,' said Lois Venning softly, earnestly. 'We need someone to help us and you seem to be different to the others who've ridden through here on their way to or from the hills.'

'Perhaps I'll come back this way when all this is over and behind me,' he said, smiling a little.

She eyed him steadily for a long moment, then shook her head, a little sadly he thought, 'No,' she said softly, her voice very quiet, 'you won't ride back this way. I know the kind of man you are. There will always be another trail beckoning you, leading on over the hill.'

'All men have to follow the trail that circumstances map out for them.'

She gave him a sharp, keen glance, arrested by his remark. 'I wonder how deep your anger really goes,' she murmured, 'whether it's such a deep-seated hatred that you'll never be able to work it out of your system even if you do find and kill the man who did this. You don't have the look of a lawless man about you and yet there is something there which frightens me a little. Are you sure that you're doing this just because this man once saved your life and you feel that you owe him something – or is it because there's something in you which drives you to do these things. There are hundreds of men like that living in these hills, existing like animals, always on the run, afraid that sooner or later the law or a bounty hunter will catch up with them, take them off guard.'

'Can anyone be sure of what lies behind his motives?'

'I think so. If he takes the trouble to really analyse his feelings. But too many men don't want to do that. They're more than content to let things go on as they are, rather than stop and try to work out why they do certain things.'

He laughed easily at that, smiling down at her from the saddle. 'I'll remember that,' he told her, 'and try to think things out like you say.'

'Now you're making fun of me,' she said, pouting a little at the tone of his voice.

He shook his head very slowly. 'No, not that,' he said sombrely. 'Stay with your first judgment of me.' Pulling on the reins, he jerked the horse's head round more quickly than he usually did, and rode out of the courtyard towards the trees that bordered the lake.

SIX

THE DEVIL'S DEPUTY

Leaving the hills behind, Rand struck out across the valley for town. He rode with a heavy heart, dulled by the burning anger in him. Reaching town, he paused for a moment at the very end of the street, seeing it all laid out in front of him. It was as if he were seeing it clearly for the first time. The bright sunlight washed over it in a harsh, golden wave, touching the walls of the buildings, forming a shimmering curtain at the other end of the street where the heat lifted from the roofs of the houses and stores.

He saw all of the meanness that was there, the signs of violence etched on either side of the street, the mistrust, anger, fear and greed that lived side by side in the town. For a moment, he felt disheartened. Was this what this great country was to come to? Or was there to be a better future for it? He knew deep within himself that if there was to be anything better, if men were to live in peace with each other, then before that could come about there had to be a period of violence during which the wild ones, the lawless element, had to be destroyed, forced out of the territory.

Reaching into his pocket, he pulled out the silver star which he had taken from Turner's body. For a long moment, he stared down at it, turning it over in his hands, the sunlight flashing brilliantly off the shining metal. Then he pinned it on to his shirt, rubbed it for a moment with his sleeve. There were several people on the main street now, although the street itself was still the boundary between the town and the gunmen's territory.

Dismounting outside the livery stable, he put his horse into one of the stalls. The groom sidled out of the shadows, a brush in his right hand. He threw Rand a quick glance, gave a bright stare at the badge, just visible on his shirt. 'You suddenly got yourself a new job, mister?' he asked. He chewed on a wad of tobacco.

'Could be,' Rand said shortly. 'You got any idea where the sheriff is at this moment?'

The other shrugged. 'Saw him makin' his way back to his office a couple of minutes ago. Don't reckon he'll like this, if you try to horn in on his territory.'

'I figure he won't be the law around here much longer,' Rand said harshly. The note of authority in his voice was clearly audible and the other looked at him with a new expression on his face.

The groom nodded slyly. 'Be careful if you start trying to stop Sutton, mister,' said the other warningly. 'He's a mighty powerful man around here, with plenty of influence. You may not get too many men to back you up if you make any move like that.'

'That's as maybe. But I'm appointin' myself acting marshal of this town as from now and if the sheriff wants to argue the point, then he'll have to do it with a gun.'

'You figurin' on seein' Mayor Carver first?'

'He likely to be in cahoots with Sutton and his crew?'

The oldster pondered that for a long moment, then shook his head. 'Don't reckon that's likely,' he said finally.

'Then maybe I'll have a talk with him first,' Rand said shortly. Going out, he made his way quickly along the boardwalk.

He found Mayor Carver in one of the small eating houses, his fat body crushed into a chair that was far too small for his bulk so that he looked permanently uncomfortable. He was perspiring freely in the heat and continually mopped at his brow, breathing heavily through his mouth. He sipped the hot coffee in front of him, eyeing Rand over the rim of the cup.

'You got any authority for settin' yourself up as marshal of this town, Kelsey?' he said at length. 'I always assumed that these appointments had to be made by the Mayor, or some other man in a responsible position.'

'That's why I came to see you first,' Rand said softly, making sure that only the other heard. 'I figure that you ought to know the way Blane has been workin'. He takes orders from Sutton and nobody else. There are men in town who're trying their damnedest to make this a decent place where people can live without fear of a bullet coming at them from the other side of the street, but they won't be able to do that until they get a lawman here who takes his orders from nobody, and answers only to his own conscience.'

'And you reckon that you're the man for the job,' said the other musingly.

'I reckon that anybody could do it better than Blanc,' Rand retorted. 'But that ain't why I'm takin' the job.'

Carver's eyebrows shot up at this. He stirred uneasily in his chair, the heavy rolls of fat on his flabby features quivering at the movement. His eyes narrowed a little. 'You're talking mighty fast, Kelsey, for a man who only rode into Willard Flats three days ago. What gives you the right to say that you're taking the post of marshal here? Could be that folk are satisfied with the way that Blane discharges his duty.'

'That may be true, but Turner was a Federal marshal. He was also my best friend and I mean to find out who killed him and exact justice. If I have to do it this illegal way by takin' his badge, then I'll do it and I wouldn't advise you, or anybody else in this town, to try to stop me.'

The other regarded him silently, speculatively, for a long moment. Then he took a thin black cheroot from his pocket, placed it carefully between his lips, and lit it by gently waving the flame of the match back and forth over the end.

'Kelsey,' he said at length, blowing a cloud of smoke into the air over his head. 'You seem to have a flair for ridin' straight into trouble. Sure as hell you'll meet up with something bigger than you can handle one of these days. Maybe this is goin' to be it, I don't know. But if you reckon that you can save this town from ruin, and I can foresee that comin' unless somebody is big enough and fool enough to stand up to Sutton and his hired guns, then the best of luck to you. Believe me, you're goin' to need it.'

'Thanks.' Rand sat back, letting his breath sigh from between his lips. He had half-expected the other to try to resist him once he pushed himself for the post of marshal in opposition to Blane. The mayor had struck him as a man who liked to retain the status quo for as long as he could, a man who disliked change if it happened to interfere with him.

'You got any idea where to start lookin' for Turner's killer?'

Rand grinned viciously. 'On the other side of the street,' he said meaningly. 'But first, I reckon I'd better pay a call on Sheriff Blane and warn him of what has happened.'

'He may not like it,' warned the other, moving his huge bulk in the confined space of his chair.

'I doubt if he will,' Rand nodded grimly. 'But if I got your authority to make arrests and hold anybody on suspicion, then I figure he'll soon find out where I stand.'

'Whatever you do, I don't want you goin' around making arrests and startin' trouble in town without any real proof,' protested the other, jerking himself forward in his chair. 'That clear?'

'Sure, I understand.'

'I know how you feel right now. Guess I'd feel the same if I'd found my best friend murdered in cold blood like that. But you can't afford to let that colour your actions. Get your proof and then do what you have to.'

'I'll do that.' Rand left the eating house hurriedly. The mayor sat quite still in his chair, watching him walk out of the place, on to the creaking wooden slats of the board-walk, pass in front of the window for a moment on his way to the sheriff's office.

Foster, coming in a few moments later, saw him and walked over, pulling back the chair which Rand had just vacated, lowering himself into it, resting his hands on the table, ordering coffee.

Carver said softly: 'There was a fast-talkin' *hombre* just walked out of here, figures he's goin' to toss Blane out of office and take over, reckons he'll be responsible for the law and order around here from now on.'

'His name Rand Kelsey?' asked the other casually.

For a moment, Carver looked surprised, then gave a ponderous nod of his head. 'That's right. You met up with him?'

'He's in bad with Sutton,' said the other, imparting the information quietly, soberly. 'Figures that Sutton had a friend of his killed.'

Carver drummed on the top of the table with his finger-tips for a moment. 'He found his friend up in the hills, buried him there. Evidently that fella Turner was a Federal marshal, came in answer to that message we sent the Governor.'

'We figured that.'

Carver nodded again. There was a broad smile on his face. 'I wonder how he will make out with Blane, and then with Sutton.'

'Seems to me that Turner was a fast man with a gun, and he died in the hills.'

'I know. But there's something about this *hombre* Kelsey that's different from most of the men I've met.'

'You mean he's got the temperament of a killer himself?'

'That could be it. When I looked into his eyes a minute

ago, I saw a dead man there.' He shivered as if the thought had struck a responsive chord in his mind. 'I didn't like it. I'm still not sure that I did the right thing in tellin' him he could take Blane's place. So long as we don't try to force Sutton's hand he seems content to let things be. I know there have been these occasional gun fights in the streets at night, but they're only isolated incidents, nothing really serious. But things could easily get out of hand if Blane goes over to Sutton and tells him of what has happened. Sutton has been relying on having a man he can talk to and order around as sheriff.'

'Maybe it's about time that things did come to a head,' said Foster thinly. 'We've been talkin' things over and we agree that we've got to stop Sutton now, before he can bring in any of those killers from the hills.'

Carver shook his head slowly. He looked distinctly unhappy at the prospect. Inwardly, he had known that a showdown would have to come sooner or later, but he was a man who kept on putting off the evil day for as long as he possibly could. Now, he felt quite sure that he had made the wrong decision when he had allowed Kelsey to walk out of the eating house with his blessing on what the other meant to do.

He gave a wry shrug of his massive shoulders. Not that he had really had any choice anyway. Kelsey would have gone through with this whether he had approved or not. At that moment, the object of his thoughts was fast approaching the sheriff's office. Sunlight glistened dully on the dust-covered windows and the door was half open. As he went up to it, he noticed Blane seated in the chair behind the long desk, his feet resting on it. The other swung his legs to the floor with a swift, almost startled, movement as Rand pushed his way in and closed the door softly behind him.

'You back in town,' he jerked out. He half rose to his feet, then sank back into his chair again. 'I figured you'd be in the hills someplace and still running.'

'Then I guess you figured wrong,' Rand said through

tightly clenched teeth. 'I rode out to try to find Jim Turner. He rode in here six weeks ago and was last seen headed for the hills.'

'And did you find him?' asked the other. Rand thought he detected a faint quaver in the lawman's voice, but he could not be sure.

'Sure, I found him all right. Shot three times in the back, and his body dragged out of sight behind a thorn bush.'

Blane jerked his head up at the hissing anger in Rand's tone. He said thickly: 'If you've got any proof who did it, then I'll check on it right away and see that the culprit is brought in for questioning and trial.'

'You'll be doin' no such thing.' Rand leaned forward over the desk, saw the sudden start of fear in the sheriff's eyes, grinned with a slight sardonic amusement as the other cringed back a little as Rand's hand went out towards his shirt. Grasping the tin badge in his fingers, Rand pulled it loose, feeling the cloth of the other's shirt tear as he did so.

'You won't be needin' this badge any longer,' he grated. 'I'm takin' over this town. You're no longer the law here.'

'You can't do that.' The other had pushed himself to his feet now, faced Rand with an angry flush on his face. 'I'm the elected representative of the law in Willard Flats and—'

'You *were* the sheriff,' Rand corrected. 'Now get out of here. I guess you'd better run to the other side of the street and warn your boss, Sutton, of what has happened.' He put just the right amount of sneering contempt into his voice. The other stiffened, his fingers twitched a little, clawed a few inches above the butt of the gun in his belt.

Rand nodded almost casually. 'Go ahead and make your play, Blane, if that's the way you want it.'

The other licked his lips dryly, then he lowered his gaze and flinched a little, backing down, wilting visibly and losing what little manhood he had left in the process. He was a beaten man, and he knew it. What pride he had left had oozed out through the pores of his skin. He had only to make a play for his gun at that moment to redeem himself. It would almost certainly have meant his own demise, but he would have retained his pride and his manhood.

For a long moment, he remained facing Rand, eyes lowered to the floor between his feet, then he whirled on his heel, moved around the side of the desk and walked towards the door, snatching his hat off the end of the desk as he did so. In the doorway, he paused, his hand on the doorknob. Harshly, with something closely akin to a sob in his voice, he snarled. 'You'll pay for this, Kelsey. Wait and see. Once Sutton learns of this, there's no place in town where you will be able to crawl and hide from what's coming to you.'

'I'll be waiting for Sutton,' Rand said ominously. 'You can tell him that from me.'

'You think you're fast with a gun.' Blane's lips were thinned back over his teeth. He seemed almost beside himself with rage. 'There are men over on that side of the street who will take you as soon as Sutton gives the word. You'll regret that you didn't take his advice and keep on riding before sundown.'

He stepped out on to the boardwalk, slamming the door behind him. Going over to the window, Rand watched the other walk slowly across the dusty street, climb up on to the boardwalk on the far side, then push open the swing doors of the saloon and pass inside. Sighing a little, he walked over to the desk and seated himself in the vacant chair. Only then did he realize that he still held the star he had ripped off the other's shirt in his hand. He stared down at it for a long moment, then hurled it into the far corner of the room where it came to rest in the dust that lay there. Fixing himself a smoke, he sat back in the chair, staring straight ahead of him, trying to put his thoughts into order. The die had been cast now. He had made his decision and there was no way of going back on his actions now.

*

Sutton had taken off his wide-brimmed hat and placed it on the saloon table in front of him when the doors opened and Blane came rushing in. He surveyed the other tautly, his eyes fastened on the man's face. Blane paused in front of the table, mouth working convulsively.

'Well,' snapped Sutton, 'what is it this time? Trouble in town?'

'Big trouble,' said the other breathlessly. 'That *hombre* Kelsey has just ridden into town and taken over as marshal. He's found Turner's body and it's his badge he's wearin' right now.'

Sutton came to his feet in an instant, lips tight, pressed into a hard line. 'What were you doin' to let him take over like that?' he snapped.

'I'm no gunman, Sutton,' Blane said tautly. 'I'm not settin' myself up against a man of Kelsey's calibre. You can get one of your boys to do it if you like, but not me.'

'All right, all right,' said the other quickly. 'We've got to go about this the right way. It's certain that he's already had a talk with Carver. Maybe I could force Carver's hand, but that wouldn't help now. No doubt Kelsey is sitting over there in your office waitin' for us to come to a snap decision and force a quick showdown with him. That will be exactly what he wants.'

'But you're not goin' to let him get away with this,' protested Blane harshly. He caught at Sutton by the arm. The other became rigid, turned his head a little to stare down at Blane's hand on his arm. 'Take your hand away from there,' he said in a thin, ominous voice.

Quickly, Blane removed his hand, straightened up again, licking his lips. 'Sorry,' he said harshly. 'Let me have a drink while we figure this thing out.' He picked the bottle from the table and poured himself a drink, tossed it down quickly, grimacing as the raw liquor hit the back of his throat.

'Let me take him,' said Colter, standing at Sutton's

shoulder. 'You owe me this after what he did before.'

Sutton turned to look at the gunhawk. 'You reckon you can take him, Colter?'

'I can take him. But it has to be my way.'

'What does that mean?'

'He's fast with a gun, crazy-fast. I want to make sure I got the advantage. I don't aim to get myself shot down in the street just so that you can have the way clear to take over this town over Kelsey's dead body.'

For a moment, there was a sharp retort balanced on Sutton's lips, then he pressed them tightly together and fought the words back. Colter was right. There was no point in taking any chances with a gunman of Kelsey's calibre. There had been little trouble with Turner. They had known where he was likely to be and it had taken them only a few seconds to shoot him down, to make sure of him. Everything would have been fine if only this *hombre* had not come riding into town and started snooping around, poking his nose where it was not wanted.

'All right. Have it your way. But I want him out of the way – and pronto. You understand?'

Colter nodded. There was a feral glitter at the back of his eyes and he ran the tip of his tongue over his lips with a terrible hunger. He said shortly: 'I've been waitin' for this for a long time. Before sundown, he'll be showing the whites of his eyes to the vultures.'

'Just be sure that you don't make any mistakes, otherwise you'll end up on Boot Hill,' Sutton told him. 'He's been forewarned by what happened to Turner. It won't be easy to get him without his gun.'

Standing outside the small restaurant which had once belonged to Ah Fong, Merriam glanced idly up and down the street in the slowly fading light. It was almost sunset and there was a fresh coolness on the street at this hour which had prompted him to come out into the open and stand there, drinking in the air and savouring the quietness which seemed to descend on the town at this hour.

Tonight, the town seemed to be more quiet than usual and he cast about him in an attempt to discern the reason for it. There was a handful of horses tethered to the hitching rail outside the Golden Belle saloon midway along the street on the other side and he guessed that Sutton and his men were parleying there, having heard by now that a new marshal had taken over the law in the town. He felt a little disturbed by this sudden turn of events himself, although he had not admitted it to anyone. Much as he knew that Rand Kelsey would be able to take care of himself, it seemed a mighty big chore for one man and as yet, he doubted if the Vigilante Committee of which he was head, would be in a position to back the marshal up whenever he made a move.

He narrowed his eyes a little as the object of his thoughts suddenly stepped into view fifty yards away, coming out of the hotel. He watched as Rand Kelsey stepped to the edge of the boardwalk, glancing in both directions, a keen and piercing glance which took in everything that could be seen. The other gave a brief nod of his head as he noticed Merriam, then stepped into the dusty street and walked across to the Golden Belle saloon.

Merriam drew in a sharp breath that whistled between his teeth. What in tarnation was the young fool up to now? he wondered tensely, walking across the street like that? Did he think he could get away with it this time, after what he had done to Blane? Even if the deposed sheriff didn't try to take a pot at him, there were plenty in there who would do it if they thought there was a chance of shooting the other in the back without too much danger to themselves; and Sutton would probably make it well worth the while for the man who killed Kelsey.

He half started across the street himself after the other, then stopped. There was nothing he could possibly do, unaided, and surely Kelsey knew what he was doing, walking into the saloon like that, quite openly and inviting trouble.

The Golden Belle saloon was more like itself at this

hour of the evening, with the barkeeps doing a brisk trade and business picking up rapidly. A small group of prospectors had arrived in town late that afternoon and were now engaged in playing poker at three of the tables. At the moment, Rand noticed as he moved slowly among the tables, they were being allowed to win modest sums, but that was something which would change quickly once their appetites had been whetted and by the time the evening was over, and they had been well plied with liquor, they would have nothing whatever left of their gold and would wake in the morning, with sore heads, lying in the gutter in some narrow alley.

But the night was young as yet and he had more on his mind than wet-nursing men who ought to know better than to play poker with crooked gamblers such as these. The strange thing was, he reflected, some of these men came back here time and time again, as if they enjoyed losing their hard-earned gold. The ways of the world were indeed curious, something he could not fathom himself.

Going over to the bar, he leaned his elbows on it and lifted a finger to the nearest of the bartenders. The man hesitated and Rand could see the look of indecision on his face. He turned his head slowly and stared across the room in the direction of Jeb Sutton who was at one of the tables, his cards held fanwise in front of his face, a cheroot clamped tightly between his teeth. Rand followed the bartender's inquiring glance, and saw Sutton look up from his cards as though feeling the other man's gaze on him. He drew his brows together as if not knowing why the man was staring at him so, then as the bartender swivelled his gaze a little, Sutton turned his head quickly, saw Rand standing there and half-rose from his chair. With an obvious effort, he controlled himself, sank back again, nodded his head very slowly.

The bartender came over to Rand, poured him a glass, made to take the bottle back with him, but Rand reached out, caught hold of it and pulled it towards him. 'Reckon if I'm to see that there's no trouble in here tonight, I ought to have a bottle with me,' he said thinly. There was a wealth of meaning in his words and the other swallowed thickly, left the bottle where it was and retreated along the bar to his former position.

Turning slowly, Rand leaned his shoulders against the solid wood of the bar, surveying the faces of the men in the room. He missed one man and let his keen-eyed glance range around the walls, seeking Colter. Strange that the other was not here, he thought. Deep down inside, he felt certain that it had been Colter who had pumped those three shots into Turner's back. How he was going to prove it was something he hadn't quite worked out yet. But it seemed highly likely that Colter had been detailed to kill him too. Sutton would not be sitting there as casually as this unless he thought he had an ace up his sleeve, ready to use it whenever he thought the moment was right. And that ace could well be Colter, somewhere out there on the loose, maybe looking for him at that moment in the streets of Willard Flats.

Pushing himself away from the bar, he made his way across the room until he stood directly behind Sutton, peering down over the other man's shoulder at the cards he held in his hand. For several moments, Sutton did not give any sign that he knew the other was there, he concentrated on the game, pushing the chips into the pile in the centre, taking the cards which were dealt him, lips pursed as he glanced down at them. But Rand could see, after a little while, that the other was beginning to feel uncomfortable. He kept running his forefinger around the collar of his shirt, trying to loosen it a little, as if it were threatening to choke him, cut off his breath.

'You got any idea where that foreman of yours is, Sutton?' Rand asked quietly, after the uneasy silence had grown long.

Without looking round, Sutton murmured: 'How should I know where he is? I don't keep him on a chain. Around the town someplace, I should think. Maybe in one of the other saloons. He's choosey about where he drinks.'

'Somehow, I don't think so.' Rand's tone remained even and flat, lacking emotion.

'Then if you know where he is, why ask me?' Sutton spoke through his teeth. He tossed his cards on to the table with a muttered curse as one of the other players took the pot.

'Because I figure that he's out there lookin' for me, maybe hopin' he can sneak up on me from behind and put three bullets into my back as he did with Jim Turner up in the hills.'

'I don't know what you're talking about. Now if you've got nothing else to say, walk on back to the bar and leave me to my game, unless you want to sit in. I don't like people lookin' down over my shoulder when I'm playing cards.'

'Why? Does it make you more nervous than you are already?'

Sutton uttered a harsh curse, swung violently in his chair until he came face to face with Rand. His features were flushed and there was an angry set to his mouth and an almost wild glitter in his eyes. 'Just what are you tryin' to do?' he grated thickly. 'If you came here to make trouble, then you came to the right place. I've got a dozen men in here who will shoot you down as soon as I lift my little finger.'

'Could be,' Rand said easily. 'But don't forget that you'll be dead before that happens.'

Some of the colour drained from Sutton's face as he sat there, staring up into Rand's eyes. It was he who looked away first. Snapping his teeth together, he turned his chair back to the table, said to the man facing him. 'Deal another hand, Harry.'

Rand smiled thinly at the other's obvious discomfiture. He stayed where he was for another moment and then went back to his original stance at the bar, poured another drink for himself. The bartender came over, stood close by him, polishing the glasses, his head lowered. He said softly, his lips scarcely moving: 'Colter was in here a little while ago, Marshal. I heard him and Sutton talking. Colter is going to take you, but when you ain't got a gun handy. He's a bad one that, cunning as a rattler. He'll probably be out yonder in one of the alleys waiting for you to ride along. Then he'll let you have it in the back.'

'Thanks for the warning,' Rand said, his voice equally low. He drank the whiskey slowly, watching everything that went on behind him, reflected in the long crystal mirror at the back of the bar.

'Blane was here too,' said the barkeep in a whisper. 'Came in when you kicked him out of his office. He ain't so dangerous as Colter, but he'll gun you down if he ever gets the chance for what you did to him. That is, if Colter don't get you first. Step careful around here, Marshal. There's trouble just waitin' to break.'

Rand smiled thinly. Out of the corner of his eye, he caught the brief reflection of a man's head and shoulders appearing for a second just beyond the swing doors. He had the feeling that it had been Colter, that the other had just glanced inside the saloon, spotted him at the bar and had then moved quickly out of sight before he could be seen. It was just possible, Rand figured, that the foreman had not realized his image would have been visible in the mirror.

Pouring a third glass from the bottle, he kept his body poised away from the bar as he did so, his gaze not leaving the mirror. For a long moment, there was no further movement beyond the doors. Had he been mistaken? he wondered. Had it been an innocent man out there, or was Colter lying in wait just beyond the doors, trying to figure out a plan to take him by surprise.

There was a sudden movement at one of the tables, distracting his glance for a second. Sutton had risen to his feet, was staring across the table at the man who had been dealing the cards. His loud voice was lifted in argument a moment later, and almost too late, Rand realized that Sutton had also seen his foreman just outside the saloon and had done this to create a diversion, to distract Rand's attention from the door.

Swiftly, he swung his gaze back. Just in time to see
Colter push the doors open and step swiftly into the room.
Rand did not move, gave no indication that he was aware
of the other's presence. He saw Colter stare at him for a
long moment. The other wasn't quite ready. Colter must
have known that even if he shot Rand in the back, in the
eyes of several of the men there, even his own compan-
ions, he would have lost stature.

Then, abruptly, a man at one of the tables on the far
side of the room, thrust back his chair and got heavily to
his feet. Rand turned slowly. He saw the fear that leapt into
Colter's eyes, saw the other make a move towards the gun
in his belt, his right hand hidden from view by his body.
Then the man who had stood up, an old prospector, Rand
noticed, said tautly: 'Hold it right there, mister.' There was
an ancient pistol in his hand and it was pointed straight at
Colter.

The foreman froze. The prospector said to Rand
although he was still keeping his eyes on Colter: 'This
hombre has got another gun in his right hand, Marshal.'

'That's what I figured,' Rand said easily. 'It's the way
men like Colter fight. If he figures he can use it, then let
him go ahead and try.'

The prospector shook his head stubbornly. 'Always like
to see a man get an even chance,' he said tightly. 'Now
drop it, mister, or I'll shoot you down myself.'

Colter's lips tightened as his mouth worked convulsively. He hesitated, then released his hold on the hidden
gun. It clattered loudly to the floor at his feet and it was
almost as if the sound had released a little of the tension
in the room. Angrily, Colter moved forward, stepping away
from the tables until he was standing in the middle of the
room. Out of the corner of his unfocused gaze, Rand
could see Sutton watching his foreman through narrowed
eyes, clearly trying to assess the other's chances.

'You came in here to make your play, Colter,' Rand said
evenly. 'When we last met, I gave you a warning. Now
you'd better back up the threats you made then, because

I'm going to kill you, Colter, make no mistake about that.'

He saw the fear leap up again in the other's eyes. He sucked in his cheeks with an almost explosive sound.

'Better make your play, Colter,' Rand said softly. He narrowed his eyes a little as he faced the other, his hands well away from the guns at his belt.

The foreman took a short step to one side, made as if to turn away and head back for the doors. Then he suddenly tensed himself, and his right hand snaked down for the gun in its holster. It had almost cleared leather before Rand's hand moved. His Colt was out and bucking in his fist as the other tried to lift his arm. He succeeded in getting off one shot that hammered into the floor at his feet before Rand's slug took him in the heart, knocking him backward on his heels. He seemed to lift up on tip-toe, took a couple of high-stepping paces backward before he went over, shoulders hitting the swing doors, knocking them open as he fell half on to the boardwalk outside the saloon.

Inside the room, nobody moved or spoke for several moments. Rand thrust the still smoking Colt back into its holster, turned slightly, picked up his unfinished drink and tossed it down swiftly. Then he walked over to where Sutton stood, knuckles leaning on the polished top of the table, his eyes wide and staring as he looked down at the dead foreman. He seemed to have realized for the first time that he had lost his fastest gun, that he was just a little more powerless than he had been a few minutes before.

Reaching down past the other, Rand picked up the card which lay face-downward on the table in front of the tall man, flipped it over, saw Sutton's gaze drawn almost unwillingly towards it. There was a tight grin on his face as he pushed his way towards the batwing doors, stepping over the prostrate body of the dead foreman. Behind him, Sutton stared down at the ace of spades.

SEVEN

THE HIRED GUN

Three days later, when the stage rolled into Willard Flats, there were only two passengers on board. Rand stood in the doorway of the Sheriff's Office, and watched them casually as they lit down from the vehicle. The first to alight was a small, balding man with a wizened, prunelike face and a heavy valise that seemed even larger than himself. He passed his glance over him, then looked at the other man who got down from the stage, stood for a few moments on the dusty street, looking about him with something more than mere casualness, as if expecting somebody to be there to meet him.

Rand's eyes narrowed as he took in the cut of the other. Dressed in city style clothes, he could have been a successful business man, were it not for the whiplike thinness of his body and the pale, snake-like eyes that ranged over everything, missing nothing of importance. As the other moved forward, his coat flipped open and Rand noticed that he wore a gunbelt slung low on his hips. As he walked forward, past the stage depot, there was a catlike crouch to his stance that told Rand everything he needed to know about the stranger who had just ridden into town and when he saw the man cross the street and go up to Sutton who was standing just outside the Golden

120

Belle saloon, engage in deep conversation with the other, he knew that Jeb Sutton had wasted no time since the shooting of his foreman and had engaged himself another hired gun.

The stage driver climbed down and moved across to Rand. 'Funny-looking cuss that one,' he said, jerking his head in the direction of the gunslinger. 'Got on at San Ramon. Never spoke a word the whole journey that I heard. Did you see that he carries guns?'

'Sure, I noticed,' Rand nodded. He rolled himself a smoke, glanced across to the saloon, but the two men had stepped inside.

'A born killer if I ever clapped eyes on one,' mused the other. He pulled at the long, silver whiskers. 'He ain't here for his own health either. See how he went right over to Jeb Sutton. I'd keep an eye on that one, Marshal. He's been brung in here to make trouble for you.'

'Funny,' Rand said, nodding, 'but that's just what I was thinkin' myself. I reckon Sutton has had to do some pretty hard thinkin'.'

'You know who that *hombre* is, Marshal?' asked the other, bird-like eyes fixed on Rand's face.

The other shook his head. 'He ain't one that I know. Could be there are some posters in the office that Blane kept as souvenirs. Not that he'd take up against a man like that.'

The driver spat into the dust, moved back to the stage. Rand paused for just a moment, then walked over to the saloon, pushed open the doors with the flat of his hands, saw Sutton and the stranger standing against the bar and crossed over to them, eyeing the man up and down with an appraising stare.

'Who's your friend, Sutton?' he asked tightly.

'That any business of yours, Marshal?' muttered the other. He seemed to have found a new confidence and there was an insolent sneer in his voice as he deliberately stressed the last word.

'If it means there's likely to be trouble in town, then it's my business,' Rand said thinly. He turned to the man standing nonchalantly by the bar. 'I don't reckon it takes much to see what sort of man you are, mister. And I ain't such a fool that I don't know why Sutton hired you.'

'Then why go around asking questions, Marshal?' put in Sutton. 'This is Wes Tyrone from San Ramon. I asked him to come here to discuss a business proposition.'

'To kill who, Sutton?'

The other's eyes drew down to mere slits and he drew in his breath sharply. He seemed to the point of making some harsh retort, but Tyrone said abruptly. 'Do I have to be here to kill anybody, Marshal? I'm interested only in settlin' down here, maybe gettin' a piece of land for myself close by, raising a few head of cattle.'

'Ain't that a little out of your line?' Rand half turned his head. 'I've heard tell of you, Tyrone. You're a hired gun. We don't want your kind here in Willard Flats. I know what Sutton may have told you. That he means to take over the town, run this territory. But he's makin' a big mistake there. He'll soon be finished here and everybody who throws in their lot with him. Better ride on out of town and keep ridin' unless you want to find yourself in the middle of the trouble when it comes.'

'I figure I'll stick around for a while, Marshal,' said the other evenly. His pale eyes never once left Rand's face. He seemed to be sizing the other up, trying to probe him for any weak spot there might be. Obviously, gunfighter that he was, Tyrone was no fool, did not take on any man unless he knew everything about him first. That was the main reason why he was still alive and there were twenty-nine notches on his guns.

Rand eyed him closely for a moment, then looked round at Sutton. 'Let me give you a little advice, Sutton,' he said. 'Don't pay this *hombre* too much to kill me. I've got a feeling he won't collect.'

*

In spite of the presence of the hired gun in town, Willard Flats retained its air of uneasy peace for three days following Tyrone's arrival. It was as if Sutton was biding his time, waiting for the right moment before he unleashed his men on the town.

Then, on the morning of the fourth day, Rand was in the eating-house, washing down his breakfast with a cup of hot coffee, when a ranny came in through the doorway, breathless.

'There you are, Marshal, been lookin' all over town for you.'

Rand eyed the other closely, then scraped back his chair and got to his feet. 'Well, you've found me,' he said evenly. 'What's the trouble?'

'Thought you might like to know that Sutton has ridden out of town with a couple of his boys. They was headed for the hills. Been some talk in the saloon last night that he's headin' out to bring in some of the hill folk.'

'Who's he take with him?'

'Jeffers and that new fella, Tyrone. They lit out in a big hurry, Marshal.'

Rand gave a brusque nod. He tightened the gunbelt by another notch, eased the guns in their holsters, then clapped his hat on his head and walked quickly out of the restaurant. Swiftly, he made his way to the office where his mount was tethered outside. Swinging up into the saddle, he was on the point of riding off when a voice hailed him and glancing round he saw Meston hurrying in his direction. The other came right up to him, stood peering up into the sunlight.

'You heading out after Sutton and those two men of his, Marshal?' he asked thinly.

Rand nodded. 'That's right. I intend to stop 'em before they get in touch with any of the wild bunch in the hills.'

'Mind if I ride along with you? I've got an old score to settle with Sutton and this is as good a time as any to do it.'

Rand bit his lower lip in indecision. Certainly he would feel better if he had another gun to back him up, and from what he had learned of this man, he knew how to handle a gun. Besides, as the other said, if there was any man in town who deserved a shot at Sutton, it was Meston. After what the other had gone through at Sutton's hands, he could be relied upon to hunt the other down, regardless of discomfort or danger.

'Mount up then,' he said tightly. 'Let's get moving. They must've got a few miles start on us and they'll be riding fast.'

As they rode out of town and headed for the broad valley that lay to the west of Willard Flats, Rand stole a quick sidelong glance at the man who rode beside him, head bent forward a little, hands gripping the reins more tightly than was necessary. Outwardly quiet, Rand gathered the feeling that there were dark things hidden in the other's mind, things which had been born and fostered in his brain by what had happened to him that night when the wagon train that had just passed through the town had been jumped by Sutton and his men. Meston had been extremely fortunate to have escaped with his life, but the experience would have left a scar on his mind that nothing but Sutton's death could efface. He smiled grimly to himself. Noticing the look on the man's face, he was glad he was not in Sutton's shoes, if the other ever caught up with him. He doubted if Sutton would die quickly or easily.

Under the growing heat of the sun, Rand sat forward in the saddle, feeling the rush of wind on his face, cooling him a little, although his back and shoulders burned where the direct rays of the sun touched them. A mile out of town, they reached a level stretch of trail and in the soft earth they picked out the hoofprints of three horses. Evidently the mounts were being ridden hard, judging by the depth of the prints. It was easy going through the valley, but once they reached the far end and began to climb towards the foothills, they were forced to push their horses at a punishing pace. Neither man spoke, each engrossed in his own thoughts.

Topping a low rise, Rand reined his mount, lifted himself high in the saddle, peered into the sunlight, along the trail that stretched away ahead of them. In the distance, high among the rocky ledges of the foothills, perhaps five miles distant, he caught a glimpse of a pale cloud of dust that marked the position of a tight bunch of riders. He pointed forward.

'There they are.' His voice was a throaty whisper. 'We'd better keep to the trees unless we want them to spot us. They may make camp in the hills and go the rest of the way in the morning. That will be our chance.'

'You goin' to sneak up on 'em after dark?' There was no emotion in the other's voice.

'I don't care how I get 'em.'

Meston nodded, but said nothing, touched spurs to his horse's flanks, and edged it towards the trees. They rode in a dark green silence, the sound of their mounts muffled by the deep bed of pine needles that had fallen over the centuries, forming a soft carpet under the trees. As they rode, Rand had the uncomfortable feeling that Sutton might be leading him into a trap. It was just a half-formed hunch in his mind and he had no definite proof of it; except that the talk about Sutton riding off to get in touch with the hill folk seemed to have been bandied around a little too freely in the saloons during the night if that ranny had managed to get wind of it. He would have thought that if Sutton really intended to bring in these killers from the hills and force a showdown, he would have done it with a little more secrecy than this. He had as good as warned the whole town of his intentions. There could only be two reasons for that. Either he considered himself to be strong enough now that he had brought in a man like Tyrone not to have to worry about

anybody knowing what he meant to do; or he had deliberately done this so that word was bound to reach Rand's
ears, knowing that the other would certainly ride out
after him and he would have the opportunity to lure him
into a trap among the hills. Perhaps, Rand reasoned, that
was what had happened to Jim Turner. Maybe he had
been fooled in this way, had ridden out after Sutton without pausing to think, believing that unless he did so,
nothing could possibly save the town. Well, it was too late
to turn back now. If he tried to do that, if he backed
down now, Meston might be tempted to go on alone and
would undoubtedly be killed and he would be looked
upon as a coward in the town. He would get nobody to
back him then, even if he tried to explain his actions.
There was nothing for him to do but to keep on riding
and keep his eyes and ears open for the first sign of trouble.

The upward trail jerked Rand back into the saddle. He
rode restlessly now. The sun was lowering quickly to the
west and some of the reds and golds were beginning to
shine through the dense growth of the trees. They had
ridden well in the timber for most of the way since cutting
up out of the valley and he felt reasonably sure in his mind
that if Sutton had not seen them during that time when
they had been forced to ride in the open, earlier in the
afternoon, he was not yet aware of their presence on the
trail at his back.

By degrees the country roughened and the pines grew
smaller and more stunted with the sharp-sided ravines
coming down from above towards them. They held as long
as possible to the crests of the long ridges, skirting the
needle-sharp boulders which thrust themselves up from
the trail. In places, the track was so narrow that they had
to ride in single file, with their legs scraping the rough
rocks on either side. Near sunset, the trees finally gave way
and they rode out into the open with the rocks piling high
on one side of the winding trail, and falling away steeply
on the other. Rand halted, motioning Meston to do like-

wise, listened intently for any sound. The deep, absolute stillness hung like the press of a heavy hand over everything.

Then, somewhere in the distance, sounds rose and fell slowly, lifted once more just as they seemed on the point of fading altogether. The faint drum of hoofbeats was clearly discernible along the trail. Meston gave a quick nod.

'It's them all right,' he said with a sharp edge to his voice. 'What are we waitin' here for?' He touched rowels to his mount's flanks, drilling it forward, but Rand reached out with a swift hand and caught at the other's bridle, hauling him up again. 'No sense in goin' in half-cocked,' he said warningly. 'The ground is too open ahead of us to push close on their trail. They'd spot us before we got within a couple of mile of 'em. We've got to play this thing careful now. I figure they'll be makin' camp in half an hour or so. It'll be dark by then and they won't want to risk ridin' the trails through the hills in the darkness. Too many fresh slides of earth for that. They'll stick with the main trail through the hills.'

'How can you be sure of that?' demanded the other harshly. 'They could turn off into any one of a dozen trails if they figured they might be followed. Then we'd never find 'em.'

'We'll find 'em once they make camp,' Rand said confidently. 'We'll take our time from now on and try not to kick up any more dust than we can help. They'll spot that long before they see us. Believe me, I want to get Sutton just as much as you do and I don't intend to let him slip through my fingers. There's far too much at stake for that.'

He led the way along the narrow trail; found the best way off the ridge. One end of this widening trail was anchored against the tall crests of the hills themselves, he reckoned and the other led straight on through them. His horse was both tired and doubtful as they came to places

where the trail had partially broken away, the dirt loose
and treacherous underfoot, causing their wary mounts to
shy violently whenever they came across a stretch like this.
Slowly, but surely, they were heading up into the hills. It
grew darker and in the fading light it was difficult to make
out obstacles clearly, and several times they were forced to
alight and lead their horses forward along stretches of
broken trail.

It took them the best part of half an hour to work their
way along the open, exposed stretch of trail. At the end of
it, they moved up into timber again and the last of the
colour faded swiftly from the western sky as they rode
forward, letting their mounts have their head, picking
their own pace. They encountered a steep-sided canyon
with water flowing swiftly at the bottom of it. The damp-
ness, lifting into the still air here where they were sheltered from the sweeping wind, assailed their nostrils and
the sound of the rushing water strengthened as the trail
dipped sharply downgrade.

At the far end of the canyon, they halted, listening for
any further sound, but there was nothing but the faint
murmur of the wind in the branches.

'They must've made camp,' Rand said softly. 'They
can't be so far ahead of us now. Another mile or so, I
reckon.'

Meston's face was grim in the dim light. He reached up
with his left hand and touched the scars that still showed
visibly on his neck. His lips were pressed together in a
tight, grim line and there was something about his attitude
that sent a little thrill through Rand's body. A man itching
to kill, he thought tensely. Whatever happened, he would
have to keep an eye on the other, or he might let his deep-
seated desire for revenge get the better of him and he
would give them away before they were ready to move in.
Against men such as Sutton and Tyrone, that could be
disastrous.

The need to run Sutton down just then was so strong
that he found it difficult to fight it down. He experienced

a quickening tightness in his veins which was almost mercury itself, then pulled himself together. They moved slowly through the thickening timber, eyes and ears alert. Here and there a creek tumbled in a rush of white foam over upthrusting rocks and a faint silver shape would sometimes flash upstream, fighting the current and the strong undertow. Opening off the trail they followed were other tracks, but these were made by animals and not by man.

Half a mile further on, he smelled smoke. It came drifting back along the trail as the wind caught it. Obviously Sutton was so sure of himself that he had lit himself a fire, made camp close by.

'We'd better go the rest of the way on foot,' Rand said in a whisper. 'One of them may be on guard. Funny they should light a fire when they must know that I'd be following 'em.'

Meston nodded, but said nothing as he dropped lightly from the saddle and tied his mount by the reins to a low branch. They moved forward together, were deep among the trees when they picked out the low murmur of voices in the distance. Rand reached out, caught the other's arm in a steel-like grip.

'Quiet!' he murmured.

Edging forward, he moved silently through the trees until the faint, flickering red glow of the fire was just visible. He peered about him in the darkness, saw no one watching the trail, felt a sense of uneasiness rising in him once more. It wasn't like Sutton not to bother to watch his backtrail. He would have done that out of sheer habit if nothing else. Once more, the feeling that this was a trap of some kind rose in his mind and it was hard to fight it down.

Meston was several feet behind him as he crawled forward on hands and knees, careful not to make a sound. Parting the brush in front of him, he looked out into the clearing where the others had made their evening camp. The fire was blazing brilliantly in the middle of the clear-

ing, sending red sparks high into the air where they were
caught up by the breeze and whirled away, fading quickly.
He made out the shapes of the three men seated around
the fire. There was the smell of bacon sizzling in the pan
over the flames, mingled with the rich aroma of boiling
coffee.

Almost without thinking, Rand rose softly to his feet,
drew the heavy .45 and went forward soundlessly on the
thick bed of pine needles, feeling them soft and springy
under his feet. He had advanced just beyond the outer
fringe of trees when Tyrone, on the other side of the fire,
glanced up and saw him. The other did not move, did not
take his eyes off him.

For a moment, there was no movement among the men
at the fire. Then Sutton seemed to sense that there was
something wrong, for he half turned and in that same
moment, Rand said: 'All right, Sutton. On your feet. The
same goes for you other two men. Any wrong move and I'll
shoot you down.'

Sutton froze as he was. He seemed on the point of
whirling and going for his gun, then obviously thought
better of it, for he moved his hands well away from his
body and heaved himself to his feet.

'Turn round,' said Rand slowly. Out of the corner of his
eye he noticed Tyrone edging his left hand towards his
belt. Thinly, he said: 'Better tell that hired gun of yours,
that unless he moves his hand back where I can see it and
comes around slowly to this side of the fire, you'll get it in
the stomach.'

'Do as he says, Tyrone,' Sutton said quickly. There was
an odd edge of terror to his voice. 'He's got the drop on
us. Don't you see that?'

Tyrone's lips were drawn back over his teeth, like those
of an animal at bay. He paused for the barest fraction of a
second, then shrugged his shoulders nonchalantly and
stepped forward.

'That's better.' The night wind scoured down the rock
wall into the clearing, its coldness reaching Rand. But his

face was still hot and sticky as he faced the others.

Raising his voice, he called: 'You there, Meston?'

The other's voice answered him almost at once from directly behind him. 'I'm here, Kelsey. We found 'em just like you said we would.'

Sutton spoke up harshly. 'Just what is this, Kelsey? Your jurisdiction doesn't extend outside of town. You got no authority to stop us on the trail like this. Besides, we're not doin' anything agin the law. You can't arrest a man for makin' camp on the trail.'

'I can if I figure why you're here,' Rand snapped.

Sutton's lips drew back into a taut smile. 'Perhaps you'd like to tell me why we're here?'

'I figure you're ridin' out into the hills to bring back some of the outlaws who infest this territory. You've got in mind riding back with 'em into town and shootin' up the whole place, then takin' it over for yourself. You've been plannin' this for a long time now. Turner tried to stop you when he found out what you were doin' and so he had to be shot in the back before he could make any more trouble for you.'

'And even if that were true, what do you think you can do about it?' Sutton was smiling broadly now.

'I can stop you permanently,' Rand said, his tone hard, flat.

Sutton shook his head. 'You made a big mistake, Kelsey,' he said smoothly. 'Do you think I'm such a fool that I'd ride out here, let you know where I was going, what I meant to do, if I hadn't taken the precaution of making sure that once you found me, as I knew you would, it would mean the end for you.'

'What do you mean by that?'

'Just that you walked into a trap, Kelsey. Like that friend of yours who tried to make trouble for me, you were so sure of yourself that you never stopped to ask who was your friend and who was your enemy.'

'You talk in riddles,' Rand snapped. 'Now shuck those gunbelts and move away from the fire. We're riding back to Willard Flats where you'll stand trial for murder.'

'Not so fast, Kelsey,' said a harsh voice behind him. 'Like Sutton says, you won't be goin' anyplace.' Meston dug his gun barrel hard into Rand's back. 'Now drop that gun or I'll blow you apart.'

Rand froze, tightened, but did not move. Meston laughed short and hard. 'It was very touching the way you fell for my story about that wagon train which was attacked, about the way Sutton and his men strung up every last one on board, me included. There was just one point you never took the trouble to check. Oh, there was a wagon train all right, and it was attacked by Sutton and his men. We did string up every man who rode with it, but this—' He came around to Rand's side, as the other dropped his .45, touched the scars on his neck, 'this was done by that band of Vigilantes in Willard Flats when they caught up with me the next morning. Guess I was unlucky. They jumped me before I knew what was happening. The rest you know, except that it was Merriam and the others who tried to string me up and left me for dead.'

'But why—?'

'Why tell you that yarn?' He laughed again and there was a wild, almost mad, look on his face. 'We reckoned that once Turner failed to send in any report that another marshal might be sent to check on things, so we arranged that somebody should fall in with any stranger riding into town. It meant I had to stay on the wrong side of the street and there was always the chance that some of the Vigilantes might decide to have another go at hanging me, but it also meant that Sutton here had an ace in the hole whenever he needed it.'

'Like right now,' said Sutton, coming forward, grinning fercely. 'With you out of the way it won't be long before that Vigilante Committee is finished.'

'You'll never get away with it,' Rand said tautly.

'No?' There was menace in the other's soft, smooth tone. 'Even if you're right, you'll not be alive to see it.'

His right hand lashed out, the fingers bunched tightly into a hard-knuckled fist. It caught Rand on the side of the head, knocking him sideways. He reeled, unable to help himself, fell against the trunk of one of the trees. Vaguely, he was aware of the other men grinning down at him as he tried to thrust himself to his feet, but before he could stand fully upright and protect himself, Sutton's boot lashed out, caught him on the side of the leg. A stab of excruciating agony lanced through his body as his leg gave way under him, pitching him to the ground. Desperately, he tried to roll out of the way of the next kick which he knew was coming. It caught him on the shin, raked along his flesh.

Rand sucked in a sharp breath, forced himself to hang on to his buckling consciousness. Whatever happened, he must not let himself go. He told himself that over and over again as he tried to get out of the way of the other's vicious kicks. Evidently Sutton was not going to be satisfied with simply killing him as he had Jim Turner. He was going to make sure that Rand suffered before the end came. A moment later, his shoulders struck the base of one of the tall trees. Gasping for breath, sucking it down into his aching chest, feeling the stabbing pain where his ribs had been kicked by the other, he managed to draw himself partly upright. Sutton was a vaguely seen, blurred shadow in front of him, with the red light of the fire at his back, so that it was difficult to see the expression on his face, although Rand caught the faint gleam of the man's teeth in the shadow of his face, and the bright glitter of killing fever in his eyes.

'Kelsey,' whispered Sutton, his lips scarcely moving. 'I'm going to make you plead for me to shoot you. Do you understand?'

His boot came up and he drove it again towards Rand's ribs, hoping to bust them completely, to maim him without killing. Watching as the other swung, Rand managed to jerk himself to one side, half falling to the ground as he

was no longer able to lean back against the trees. But
Sutton, missing his swing completely, yelled loudly in pain
as his foot struck the tree, throwing him off balance. He
fell heavily, somehow managed to get to his feet as Tyrone
moved in, motioned with the Colt in his hand as Rand
made to leap on Sutton.

'Get back,' Tyrone whispered. 'I figure Mister Sutton
has other plans for you, so I don't want to have to plug you
now, but I will if I have to.'

Rand sank back. No sense in inviting a bullet, he
thought dully. If he managed to stay alive, it was just possible he might get a chance to turn the tables on these
men.

Sutton dragged breath as he got to his feet, glared
down at Rand. 'Just for that, I'll drag things out a little,'
he promised. He turned to Tyrone. 'Keep an eye on him
while we eat. After supper, I'll decide what to do with
him.'

'Sure thing.' Tyrone grinned viciously. He moved a
few feet away from where Rand lay, squatted on a low
rock, the .45 held calmly in his right hand. He dug into
the pocket of his shirt, pulled out a tobacco pouch and
opened the strings with his teeth, not once taking his
gaze off Rand. Placing the Colt on the rock beside him,
he smiled.

'Just try,' he said blandly, as though divining Rand's
thoughts. 'That's all I ask.'

Rand lay where he had fallen, breathing hard, trying
to force the nausea from his stomach. His chest ached as
if every rib in his body had been broken, but as he felt
them gingerly, he discovered that although they were
probably badly bruised, there were no bones broken – as
yet. He did not doubt that Sutton would have plenty
more punishment in store for him and he cursed
himself fiercely for not having checked on Meston a
little more thoroughly. It was his own fault that he had
fallen into this trap. He had been too ready to accept
what the other had told him. Perhaps if he had even

taken the trouble to ask Merriam about him, he would have found out long before just where Meston's sympathies lay.

The men ate their supper, scarcely bothering to glance in his direction. Meston took a plate and a cup of coffee across to Tyrone, then went back to the fire. They conversed together in low voices and although Rand was able to pick out only snatches of conversation, he guessed they were discussing how to get rid of him.

Finally, Sutton got to his feet. It gave Rand a sense of pleasure to see that he staggered as he walked over to him. That blow on the knee when he had fallen had pained him.

'Now I'm goin' to bust you real good, Kelsey,' he said, standing over him. He kicked again at Rand's chest. The pain came surging up through his body, riding on a crest of nausea that bubbled up into his throat and brought a foul, bitter taste of vomit into his mouth. He tried to hold it in, feeling the colour drain from his face, and the sweat start out on his forehead.

'I know plenty of ways I've never tried on a man yet,' Sutton said viciously.

'Indian ways, I guess,' Rand said through tightly-clenched teeth. He fought to keep the agony from overwhelming him.

Sutton almost went berserk at that. He continued to kick Rand in the chest and on the legs until he was swaying. Then he bent and began to strike him hard with his tightly-bunched fish. The blows came thick and fast. Rand tried desperately to move his head out of the way of the other's swinging arms, but it was impossible to ride them all on his arms and shoulders and long before the other had finished, his face was raw and bleeding and there was a vast and throbbing ache in his skull that threatened to engulf him in a sea of pain.

Sutton was almost spent now. His fury was still there, but his strength was oozing out of his arms where they hung loosely by his sides.

Tyrone came forward from where he had been sitting on the rock watching the proceedings through interested eyes. He said: 'Let me finish him, Sutton.'

'No.' The other spoke sharply. 'He hasn't suffered enough yet. But in his present state he hardly knows what is happening to him. We'll wait until he's fully conscious again.' Turning, he put his knee in Rand's face as he moved away and the blackness came in to engulf him.

When he finally came round, the blackness was still there, apparently deep and never-ending. He tried to come out of it, fought his way to the surface and knew pain once more. His body was a mass of bruises, scratches and blood. He tried to move his head very slowly, sucked air down into his lungs as pain lanced through his head and neck muscles. He almost passed out once more, felt the unconsciousness coming and going, like waves breaking on the grey shores of his brain.

There was something grinding into the small of his back, forcing him to be aware of it. With an effort, he forced his eyes open, tried to see around him. Redness flickered and wavered on the very edge of his vision but several seconds fled before he realized what it was. He was facing away from the fire in the clearing and he was seeing the fainter reflection of the flames on the leaves and branches of the trees ten yards away.

Very cautiously, he turned his head, forcing himself to ignore the pain in his head and neck. The four men were seated around the fire now, conversing in low tones. Evidently, they considered him to be still unconscious, knew that he would not be able to get away from there, that one of them would be able to shoot him in the back if he tried to make a run for the trees. And in his present weakened condition, he would be unable to make any progress at all through the brush even if he did succeed in gaining the shelter of the timber.

Slowly, he inched his way to one side, sliding his body off the stone that seemed to be grinding into his back. He moved his right arm, felt for it, then felt a sudden surge of hope as his fingers closed around the object, discovered that it was not a stone as he had first thought, but the Colt he had dropped when Meston had crept up on him from behind. Somehow, in the struggle since then, it had been overlooked by the others.

Closing his fingers around it, he drew it up towards him. The others were still at the fire, had apparently noticed nothing.

Very slowly, an inch at a time, he pushed himself up until he was in a sitting position, facing the fire. There was a tremendous weakness in him and the blood had rushed, pounding sickly, to his head, so that the whole clearing, the fire, and the dark figures of the men seated around it, seemed to tilt and sway in front of his vision. Somehow, he forced his vision to right itself. Hard-faced and hard-eyed, thrusting down the weakness that threatened to sweep over him once more, he faced the men at the fire, said in a hoarse tone: 'All right, Sutton. Turn round slow and easy or I'll kill you right now.' Relishing it, he allowed himself the luxury of drawing down on the big man real slow, but keeping an eye on the other three men at the same time.

Sutton uttered a harsh curse. He half rose to his feet, mouth twisting as he tried to put his thoughts into words. On the other side of the fire, Meston whirled, threw himself to one side with a loud yell, tugging at the gun in its holster. Rand fired instantly, swinging the Colt slightly. Meston seemed to jerk upright, even as he was falling. Then he slumped back over the rock near which he had been sitting. His head was thrown back so that the firelight fell full on it, highlighting the bones of his cheeks, the wide, staring eyes, and the red stain that spread slowly on the front of his shirt as the gun slipped from nerveless fingers.

For a moment there was complete silence, Sutton turned his head very slowly and stared round at the dead man as though unable to believe that anyone could be so fast and accurate. Then he called loudly: 'Get him, Tyrone!'

The words were scarcely out of his mouth when he, too, dived forward, reaching for his gun, and as if it had been a pre-arranged signal, the remaining two men moved swiftly, jerking themselves away from the fire as they did so.

Rand kicked himself to one side, twisted in mid-air and fired even as he hit the ground. A bullet scorched into the earth less than two inches from his head and another plucked viciously at his sleeve, burning along his forearm. Jeffers died as he tried to get to his feet, swaying drunkenly forward, clutching at his belly as he fell. His body crashed into the fire, scattering the logs and burning branches in all directions, the iron pot with the coffee bubbling in it tilting and spilling its contents on to the flames.

Sutton scuttled behind the rocks, crouched down out of sight. On the other side of the clearing, Tyrone had thrown himself down in a shallow depression and sent a couple of shots close to where Rand lay. Rand felt the breath of the slugs and pushed himself closer to the ground, snapping a quick shot in Tyrone's direction as he did so. He heard the other yell out, saw the man jerk his head sharply to one side, had a fragmentary glimpse of the long, bloody streak down the other's face where the slug had torn deeply through his cheek. Rand felt an inward sense of satisfaction. If nothing else, that would mean that Tyrone was marked for life, he thought fiercely.

From behind the rocks where he lay, Sutton yelled harshly. 'Kill him, Tyrone. That's what I've paid you for.'

Rashly, the other edged from behind the rocks and tried to get in a shot at Rand himself. For just a fraction of a second, he was in full view of the other, with the firelight shining directly on his face. Jerking his weapon around, Rand fired once. Sutton seemed to remain kneeling on the ground for what seemed an eternity. For a moment, Rand felt sure he had missed with that shot, and lifted his gun again, finger tightening on the trigger as he aimed to get in another shot at the other. Then he paused, relaxed the pressure on the trigger as Sutton bent forward, the whole of his long body sliding into view as he fell forward on to his face.

For a moment, silence lay over the clearing. Then Rand called harshly: 'Sutton is dead, Tyrone. Now it's your turn.'

For a moment, nothing happened. He scanned the area where he had seen the gunman go to ground. The roaring of blood in his head increased to a dull, surging pain and he could sense the darkness coming in on him once more, knew that he had not to give way. Not with a killer like Tyrone waiting out there on the edge of the orange fireglow, waiting to get in a killing shot at him.

There was a sudden movement on the very edge of the clearing and he saw what he had begun to suspect. Tyrone leapt suddenly to his feet, several yards from where Rand had last seen him. He whirled swiftly, loosed off one shot, knew that he had missed. Then he heard the other crashing his way through the brush, back towards the trail. Staggering a little, weakened by loss of blood and the beating he had received at Sutton's hands, he moved towards the trees, reloading the chambers of the gun. He had almost reached them, was on the point of plunging forward into the tangled underbrush, when he caught the sound of a horse being ridden hard along the trail.

There was no chance of catching up with Tyrone now, he thought dully. The chances were that the gunman would take the trail which led over the mountains and keep on riding once he hit the other side of the range. With Sutton dead there was nothing to keep him here in the territory.

Going back to the fire, he bent over the three bodies, made sure they were all dead, then sank down on to his haunches, staring into the dancing flames. Reaching forward, he picked up the coffee pot, found that there was still a little left in it and poured it into a cup, gulping the scalding hot liquid down even though it burned his throat on its way to his stomach.

His chest and back were one steady throb and he knew times of sickness and pain during the long night. He slept most of the time and when he woke from a dreamless doze, it was to find the sun already lifting high in the east, throwing its light into the clearing, with the fire burned down to grey ash and a few glowing embers. He tried to make something to eat, knew that he would have to get away from there soon. But when he tried to get to his feet, his legs gave way under him and he fell forward, unable to resist the dragging darkness which swamped him. Everything was a blur of darkness, of stabbing pain and then a long slide down into nothingness.

EIGHT

THE GUNFIGHTER

He was aware if a blur of pain and weakness, of sickness that rose in his stomach and threatened to choke him, of fever and sweat that lay on his body. Then there was something else. He seemed to hear voices, a long way off, coming closer and then fading again, a woman's voice and a man's which spoke at less frequent intervals. He had the vague feeling of being lifted, of sitting astride a horse that moved slowly and more smoothly than any horse he had ever known, of cold water being poured gently down his parched throat.

He knew that he made sounds, tried to speak, to cry out but a hand touched his shoulder and held him back whenever he tried to move. How long it was before he opened his eyes again, he did not know. He had the feeling that an eternity had passed and yet that did not seem to be possible. When he opened his eyes, he expected to see the fire burning once more in the clearing among the rocks and trees, to see those four men seated around it, feel the hard shape of the Colt in his hands.

But the light that fell on his eyes was pale and diffuse, yet steady. Not firelight. Sunlight, filtering through curtains into the room, falling on the bed where he lay with his back and shoulders against cool sheets and his head on a soft pillow. He had to be dreaming, he told himself numbly. This could not be really happening to him. Possibly something brought on by a delirium, by the fever. Then something was placed to his lips and he felt a cooling liquid trickling into his mouth and down his throat.

The sickness came again in spite of everything he could do to prevent it. He wanted to keep that liquid down because it cooled the raging fever in his body and assauged the terrible thirst. But even as that thought crossed his mind, the darkness returned and he knew nothing more for another unguessable eternity. This time, he felt a little better, a little stronger in himself. He was able to keep his eyes open without the stabbing agony lancing through his forehead and back into his brain. It was dark, but then he noticed a pale yellow glow, turned his head on the pillow and saw the girl bending over him, the candlelight at her back making a warm halo of her hair.

'You're awake at last,' she said softly, her voice gentle and rich. 'You've been ill for a long time.'

'What happened to me?' he asked weakly, lips forming the words almost of their own volition.

'We found you up in the hills five days ago. Your horse and another were tethered to a tree along the trail but there was no sign of you, so we went on into the clearing and that was where we found you.'

'We?' he asked.

'My father and I,' she explained. 'We managed to get you on to your horse and brought you back here to the ranch. You've been delirious ever since.'

He put up a hand and rubbed his forehead. 'I dimly remember the gunfight,' he said harshly. 'Sutton beat me up after Meston had betrayed me.'

'You don't have to worry about them any longer,' she said, her voice holding a strange tautness. 'They're both dead, along with another man I don't know.'

'Jeffers. One of Sutton's men. But what about Tyrone?'

'Who?' She looked at him with a puzzled frown puckering her lips.

'He was the hired gun that Sutton brought into town. He paid him to kill me. I got a shot at him, but he managed to get away.'

'He's probably riding for the border now,' she said. 'But you'd better lie back until the doctor has another look at you tomorrow morning.'

He made no protest, but lay weakly back on the pillow and closed his eyes. This time, the blackness of unconsciousness did not come and he fell into a deep and natural sleep.

When he woke the next morning he felt different, stronger, and there was the feeling in his mind that it was good to be alive. He opened his eyes wide, looked about him. The bedroom was empty, but a moment later, the door opened and Lois Venning came in, saw that he was awake and came over to his bedside. 'I'm making you something to eat,' she said softly, arranging his pillow. 'I thought you might be feeling better today. You slept soundly all through the night.'

She brought him soup a little while later, hot and with pieces of meat and sweet potato floating in it, fed him with a spoon even though he protested that he was now quite capable of feeding himself.

Later that morning, she came back with a stranger, a short, white-whiskered man who placed his bag on the small bedside table, felt Rand's pulse, made him put out his tongue, then checked the bandages which had been wound tightly around his chest. Finally, he nodded his head without saying anything.

'Well, Doc?' Rand asked sharply. 'When can I get up and leave this bed?'

'You can get up for a while tomorrow,' said the other, rising to his feet and closing the bag with a snap. 'But that's all. If you've got any ideas of leaving here and riding back to town you can forget them for another week.'

Rand sighed. There was something in the other's tone that brooked no argument.

'Sutton is dead,' he said softly, leaning back. 'I suppose you know that by now.'

'Yes, I know. I guess the whole town knows.'

'Has there been any more trouble?'

'None that I know of. Merriam swears he'll run the rest of Sutton's men – what few there are still in town – out if they don't go peaceable. He means it too. You've started something, young man.' There was a note of warmth in the doctor's voice. 'Now just get some rest. That's all you need now. I've done all I can for you. Nature will do the rest if you give her a chance.'

It was another six days before he was well enough to leave the ranch. He knew that Lois Venning did not want him to go, but he had to get away, get back to town and see for himself what had been happening there while he had been away. He had grown to suspect that the doctor was not telling him everything of what was happening in Willard Flats and the thought began to worry him more than he cared to admit, even to himself.

Now he stood in the small courtyard, looking about him, savouring the sight of the tall hills in the near distance, of the clear waters of the lake where they were just visible through the tall, slender trunks of the pines. This was sure a wonderful place, he thought inwardly; a man could settle down here, put down roots and live for the rest of his life in the quietness of the hills. He shrugged the thought off with an effort. No point in thinking along those trails, he told himself. His was a wandering life, a roving nature, and he doubted if there was anything that would change that, whether he wanted it to or not.

The girl came out on to the porch, stood looking down at him. 'You getting ready to leave?' she asked, her voice low.

He nodded slowly. 'I have to go,' he said, making it

sound as though he was having to defend his decision. 'I want to know what is happening in town.'

'Do you have to?' There was a strange quality to her tone now and she stepped down into the courtyard, came to stand closer to him. 'You don't owe them anything now. You've paid in full for anything they may have done for you. Don't you see that you're free now, free to choose any trail you want. They have no hold on you, these men in Willard Flats. You only took that job as marshal because of what happened to your friend in these hills. But you've avenged that now. What more do you have to do?'

'I wish I knew. Maybe I have to drive this restless urge out of me. Until I succeed in doing that, I guess I'll never be really free. No matter where I go or what I try to do.'

She shook her head as though exasperated with him, as if he were a child that needed scolding. 'I wish I could make you see,' she said, suddenly helpless. 'What will you do once you've seen all there is to see in Willard Flats? Ride on again, taking any trail that leads you on to the horizons? That isn't the sort of life for a man like you.'

'You don't know what sort of man I am,' he told her. He lifted his gaze to where the valley swept out, down from the hills, widening away into the sun-hazed distance.

'I think I do,' she said softly. 'I've nursed you for eight days when you were as close to death as any man I've seen. I know what you are.'

'Then you know why I have to go back,' he said stubbornly.

She stared at him for a long moment, lower lip pouting a little. Then she gave a quick little nod. Turning, she ran quickly into the house. Rand stood there for a long moment, feeling the coldness in him, knowing now what was his for the taking, but knowing that he could not do so.

He went into the small barn, picked his horse out of the stall to the rear and led it out into the open. Fetching his saddle from where it lay against the wall, he placed it over the horse's back, tightened the belly strap under the animal, then straightened up slowly. He worked quietly with his gear, tightening it into place, checked the Winchester, pushed it back into the oiled leather of the scabbard.

'Riding out?' Venning stood behind him, his face bearing a serious expression.

Rand nodded. 'Figured it was time I stopped playing on your hospitality and headed back for town,' he said. 'I may have some unfinished business there.'

'What makes you think that?' asked the other, eyeing him closely.

Rand shrugged. 'Just because Sutton is dead don't mean to say that the rest of his men will have left town. They may still figure there are plenty of rich pickings to be made off the prospectors who come in for supplies and if they find a way of doing it without the law stepping in and puttin' a stop to it, then the town could slip back into its old ways pretty quickly. Might even get somebody there even worse than Sutton was.'

'Wish you'd stay here. I need a hand around the place and—' He broke off.

'Wish I could.'

'You be headin' back this way sometime, when you've finished your business in town?'

'Could be.' Rand nodded, then swung up into the saddle, sitting tall and straight for a long moment, wondering if Lois would come out of the house to say goodbye, but there was no sign of her and almost sharply, he pulled the horse's head around and rode quickly out of the courtyard, heading east into the valley.

His horse's hoofs made hollow sounds on the bridge outside of town and they seemed to echo the feeling inside his own mind. He felt fully recovered from his recent ordeal now; a little thinner perhaps, but that was all. The silver star was still on his shirt, half hidden by his jacket. It was high noon when he rode into town and the street was almost deserted. Siesta time, with most of the folk indoors or in the saloons, slaking their thirst, washing the dust of the trail from their throats.

He halted in front of the sheriff's office, went inside. Even as he stepped into the outer office, he grew aware that someone was already there. His hand was dropping instinctively towards the gun at his waist when he hesitated as he recognized Merriam. There was a look of surprise on the other's face. He got up from behind the desk, came around it, his hand outstretched. His grip was genuine.

'Never figured you'd come riding back into town, Kelsey,' he said warmly. 'But I'm sure glad to see you. Blane has been tryin' to get his old job back, but without any luck so far. We heard about what happened, knew you were at the Venning place.'

'I reckon I'd have died if it hadn't been for Lois Venning and her father,' he said, sinking gratefully into the chair behind the desk, putting his feet up. 'But with Sutton out of the way, it shouldn't be too difficult for you to clean up the town.'

Merriam's face assumed a more serious expression. He said slowly. 'I'm afraid it isn't quite as simple as that.'

'No? Why not?'

'Well . . . I suppose you've got to know sometime, it's that—'

'All right, spit it out.' Rand lowered his feet to the floor, sat forward in his chair, resting his elbows on the top of the desk. 'What's on your mind?'

'That gunhawk, Tyrone.'

'What about him?' Rand spoke through thinned lips.

'He's in town. Rode in a few days ago. He's passing word around that he means to kill you the minute you show up.'

'So that's it.' Rand pondered it. He let his breath come out through his nostrils in slow pinches. There was a direct look from Merriam with something real sharp at the back of it. Something keen and wise, very seeing and knowing. He must have guessed what was in Rand's mind, for he said quickly, 'He's a tricky customer, Rand. He may call you out in fair fight, believing that he's faster than you are, or he may sneak up on you from behind in the dark and shoot you in the back. But you marked him for life. He'll never rest until he's avenged that.'

Rand remembered the slug of his which had torn through the other's cheek back in that clearing among the hills and he knew that Merriam was speaking the truth on that point anyway.

'If he wants a showdown he can have it,' Rand said soberly.

'Don't take any chances with this gunman,' said the other warningly as he moved towards the door. 'He has killed twenty-nine men already so they say.'

'There has to come an end to everything,' Rand declared enigmatically. He sat back, deep in thought, as the other opened the street door and walked out, closing it softly behind him. Rand heard his footsteps on the wooden boardwalk fade into the distance.

There was a tightness in him that he did not like and be hunted around in the desk until he found Blane's private store of whisky, brought out a glass and poured himself a drink, gulping it down, coughing a little as the raw liquor touched the back of his throat. But it brought an expanding haze of warmth and feeling back into his stomach and he felt a little better. Through the dusty window, he was able to make out a small bunch of men on the opposite sidewalk, but none of them was Tyrone. He wondered whether the hired gun knew he was back in town or not. Somebody must have seen him ride in and would have passed the word to the other by now, he reasoned.

He poured a second glass but left it untouched on the desk in front of him. There was a whole host of ideas rushing around in his head, each crying out for his undivided attention. He tried to put them into some form of order. His mouth increased its firmness and he sat back to roll himself a cigarette. He relished the smoke, felt it send its warmth and energy through him. Outside, sunlight moved overhead. Pretty soon, the heat would fill the basin in which Willard Flats lay and the dust would hang heavy in the air. Sitting back, outwardly relaxed, he turned events over in his mind. He was still seated there, the smoke almost finished, engrossed in his thoughts, when the door opened and Mayor Carver came in, waddling forward after shutting the street door behind him. He mopped his brow as he sank down gratefully on to the low couch at the far side of the room.

'Heard you was back in town, Kelsey,' he allowed softly. 'Just met Merriam along the street.' He glanced idly through the window. 'Sure is goin' to be hot today. Dust blowing up too.'

Rand eyed him curiously. 'You didn't come here just to tell me that,' he said. 'You got somethin' on your mind? If so, let's have it.'

'Well, now, ain't an easy thing to put into words, specially seeing what you did for the town, gettin' rid of first Colter and then Sutton.'

'Forget about what I did,' Rand told him harshly. 'I did all of that for Jim Turner, not for the town.'

'Glad you look at things that way.' Carver let his hands rest on his knees. He still looked troubled, brows pulled tightly together until they formed a straight, continuous line across his eyes. 'Now that both Sutton and Colter are dead, I figure that just about winds things up as far as you're concerned. You won't want to stay around here any longer. Those rannies on the other side of the street will drift on over the hills in a little while, I've seen it happen before. Soon as they lose their leader, they break up, drift apart, go look for new pastures. Sure, we may still have the gamblers here to take care of the prospecting folk who come down from the hills, but I figure we know how to handle them.'

'Then what's on your mind?'

Carver stared right at him for a long moment, licked his lips slightly, then muttered: 'You, Kelsey!'

Rand experienced a little start of surprise, stared at Carver. 'Where do I fit into all this?' he demanded hoarsely. Dropping the butt of his cigarette on to the floor he ground it out with his heel, sat back in the chair, regarding the other curiously.

'Two ways, Kelsey.' Carver leaned forward earnestly, seemed to be having some difficulty getting his thoughts shaped into words. 'No offence meant here, of course. We got nothin' against you personally, but—'

'Go on,' said Rand drily. 'Just what is it you're tryin' to say?'

Carver wiped his face again, tugged uncomfortably at his wing-collar for a moment. 'Blane is still chagrined at the way you threw him out of his job. When we heard somethin' of what had happened up in the hills, he came along to see me and asked for it back. I told him that if Sutton was dead, then I saw no reason why he shouldn't have it. Just try to see my side of this. He's no killer, Kelsey. Sure he used to let things slide and he may have been biased a little on Sutton's side, but I reckon if he'd tried to stand up to Sutton, this town would have blown right up in our faces. Now that Sutton's gone, I figure he might make us a better sheriff than before.'

'And the other reason?' With a tremendous effort, Rand succeeded in keeping the hard stirring of anger down.

'It's Tyrone. That hired gun is still roamin' around town like a mountain cat waitin' for its prey. We heard he got away from the fight. He came high-tailin' it back here some days ago.'

'He got his money from Sutton. Even if he didn't carry through his side of the bargain, he should be satisfied. Sutton won't be wantin' any change now.'

'It ain't the money that's troublin' him. You seen his face, Kelsey?' Carver shook his head slowly, sweat glistening on it. 'No, I see you ain't. It's far from pretty, believe me. He was no oil paintin' before, but he's far worse now. This is a personal matter he means to settle with you. It's got nothing to do with Sutton or anybody else. Just the two of you. We figure that if you were to leave town, pull out right now, it might help solve both our problems.'

Slowly, Rand eased his body forward in the chair. 'You suggestin' that I should turn and run, Carver?' He spoke flatly, tight-lipped.

Carver spread his hands. 'I know how it sounds, Kelsey. But you've got to see things our way. Tyrone is a killer. If you stay around in town, he'll come lookin' for you, may even take Sutton's place if he manages to outdraw you. We know he's fast and he's already killed plenty of men, some of 'em fast guns too. Those rannies yonder might think twice about ridin' over the hill and they may just get steamed up enough to follow him.'

'You sure scare easy, Carver.' Rand's voice lashed the other mercilessly, savagely and he saw him wince under the naked scorn in it. 'If Tyrone wants a showdown, he knows where to come lookin' for me. Tell him that if you see him. He's got until sundown to get out of Willard Flats. The stage leaves at four o'clock from the depot. If I don't see him gettin' on it, I'm goin' lookin' for him myself.'

Carver sighed. 'That your last word, Kelsey? Remember, you ain't a properly authorised marshal. That badge may mean a lot to you, but in law it means exactly nothin'.'

Rand felt the anger boiling in him, threatening to overwhelm him, direct his actions into channels of violence. Fists clenched, he got to his feet, faced the other over the desk. 'You'd better get out of here, Carver,' he said thinly. 'Seems I forgot this town was a place of little, shallow people with short memories. Little men who are scared of their own shadows, jumping for cover like a bunch of jack rabbits whenever there's any sign of trouble on the street. You don't seem to realize that if you want to make this into a place where decent men and women can live in peace, without the risk of being shot at from the dark, you've got to fight for it. So far, seems I did all of the fighting. Now that you figure you've got most of what you want, I'm to ride on out, to become a little, frightened man like the rest of you.'

'You got no call to talk to me like that,' quavered the other hesitantly, his heavy, fleshy jowls quivering with a mixture of fright and righteous indignation. 'As mayor here I have to think of the good of the town and—'

'You think of nothin' but the good of yourself, Carver,' said Rand angrily. 'Now get out of this office before I really lose my temper and throw you out.' He came around the edge of the desk and advanced ominously on the other. Carver heaved himself up from the low couch with a lot of creakings and groanings of springs, moved to the door with a rapidity that belied his bulk. In the doorway, he paused, opened his mouth as if to say something further, then ran out as Rand walked towards him, hurried along the boardwalk, almost tripping over his own feet in his anxiety to get away. Rand watched him out of sight, then closed the door of the office, hitched his gunbelt a little higher around his middle and stepped down into the middle of the hot, dusty street. His eyes roved in every direction as he made his way slowly down the main street of Willard Flats, feeling a little tension begin to grow all around him. Out of the corner of his vision, he noticed the faces which were pressed momentarily at the windows of the buildings overlooking the street, faces which would be hurriedly withdrawn whenever he turned his head to stare directly at them.

Women with children, standing gossiping in the shop doorways, would hurriedly shoo their children into the shops. Opposite the Golden Belle saloon, he paused, then turned and walked inside. Several of the rannies standing near the doorway moved away as he brushed past them, his eyes flicking over the face of each man there, but he saw nothing of the man he sought.

Going up to the bar, he said loudly: 'You know where I can find Tyrone? I hear he's been lookin' over town for me.'

'Hasn't been in here today, Marshal,' said the barkeep hesitantly. 'You want me to give him any message if he does come in?'

'Just tell him I'm waitin' for him whenever he wants to make his play.'

'Sure, Marshal, sure.' The other nodded his head hurriedly, his gaze flicking from one side of the room to the other. 'I'll do that for you.'

'Now pour me a beer,' Rand said, nodding. 'Get's mighty hot out there in the street lookin' for a low-down killer like Tyrone.' He spoke deliberately, knowing that sooner or later, one of the rannies there would meet up with the hired gun and tell him all that had happened. The beer was cool when it arrived and slaked his thirst far better than whiskey would have done. He ordered another, stood with one elbow resting on the bar, turning towards the men in the saloon, noticing the looks of sullen resentment on their faces. Every one of them was hoping that when Tyrone and he met face to face, the gunman would kill him. He felt a twist of grim amusement in his mind.

'Now that Sutton is dead, I reckon there'll be no call for you men to stay around town any longer,' he said tightly. 'If you want to stick around, then you obey the law. If not, then just get your horses and ride on out.'

No one said a word as his cold, clear gaze swept over them. But he knew that once Tyrone was dead, his orders would be obeyed. Like wolves that ran with a pack, they needed a leader and without one, they disintegrated, became lone animals, continually on the run until a bullet caught up with them someplace. All he wished now was an even chance at Tyrone, a straight encounter. He wanted nothing more and knew he would be satisfied with nothing less. This was another obligation in his life, something that had come up, not of his own asking, but because of the way events had turned out.

The bitterness welled up in him as he remembered Jim Turner, the old savage desire to set himself against these men who lived by the gun, who never gave a man an even chance, but shot him in the back from cover. Tyrone had been brought in to kill him, had received blood money from Sutton to do just that. Now events had altered even this. In ordinary circumstances, with Sutton dead and

unable to reclaim the money, Tyrone would probably have
been willing to ride on out of town, his mission unfulfilled.
He was a gunfighter, not a senseless man, and if he could
earn his money without risking his neck, then he would do
so. But that bullet which Rand had fired and which had
scarred his face for life, had also scarred his mind and this
was, as Carver had said, a personal feud between the two
of them.

Finishing the beer, he moved away from the bar,
pushed his way through the men near the door, went out
into the sunlit street. The dust which had been blowing up
for the past hour, was now thick in the air, borne along by
the stiff wind that howled along the street, blowing balls of
tangled mesquite in front of it, sending them rolling on to
the boardwalks, where they came to rest against the
wooden walls of the buildings.

Lowering his head, he moved forward into the teeth of
the wind, feeling the hot grains of dust beat against his
face like a multitude of tiny fists. It worked its way into
everything, down the collar of his shirt, itching and irri-
tating on his flesh. It would blow itself out eventually, he
reckoned, but not before it had brought a long afternoon
and evening of discomfort to everybody in Willard Flats.

On the high side of town, the sound of a horse came
along, rapid and loose. The slightly ragged pace of a tired
mount that was being pushed to the limit. The rider
broke into view at the head of the street, bending forward
in the saddle, a grey and not wholly distinct shape, half
hidden by the swirling dust. Rand stood still, half recog-
nizing the other but it was not until the man saw him and
reined his mount to a standstill that he saw it was Matt
Blane. The other was halted less than ten feet away, sitting
forward a little in the saddle, bent with the wind at his
back. His eyes were narrowed down to mere slits.

'I been riding the hills lookin' for you, Kelsey,' he gritted, voice rasping from the depths of a parched throat.
'Never figured on lookin' for you back in town. Now
you're goin' to pay for what you did.' He eased himself

back, hands resting just above the guns at his waist. 'Jerk
your iron, Kelsey.'

Rand smiled thinly. 'Don't be a fool, Blane. You know I
can shoot you down before you get that iron of yours clear
of leather.'

He saw the other hesitate as the truth of it bit home to
him, but he was too filled with anger and the desire for
revenge for it to make any lasting impression on him and
Rand knew that the other was going to call him out.

Then, abruptly, a fresh voice from behind him said:
'Leave him be, Blane. This one is mine.'

Tyrone's voice. The gunman went on more softly. 'Just
turn around nice and slow, Kelsey. I want you to be facing
me when I put a bullet into you. Try for your guns if you
want to, but it won't do you no good. Just send you into
eternity that mite quicker.'

Rand stood quite still, estimating exactly where the
other was from the sound of his voice. The other was a
little too confident, reckoning that now he had the drop
on Rand, he could afford to take his time in shooting him
down.

'Turn around, Kelsey.' The other lifted his voice a little
and Rand guessed he was standing close to the boardwalk,
less than twelve feet away. 'You goin' to turn around,
Kelsey, or do I have to plug you in the back?'

For a moment, Rand relaxed. Then, abruptly, he
whirled, dropping and drawing his guns as he did so. The
Colts bucked in his hands as he went down. He heard the
hum of a bullet close to his head, saw the gunman standing
almost exactly where he had placed him from his voice.
Tyrone seemed to be having difficulty in standing upright.
It was almost as if he were swaying into the wind, knees
bending a little, eyes wide open as he fought to keep the life
in them. Then he dropped to his knees, the blood gushing
from his mouth with every exhalation. Slowly, he toppled
forward, the look of surprise still stamped on his features.

Holstering one of his guns, Rand turned to face Blane,
felt a stirring of stunned surprise as he found himself look-

ing down at the body of the ex-sheriff, one foot still entangled in the stirrup, his hair trailing in the dust.

Going forward, Rand bent to examine the other, knew then what had happened. One of Tyrone's shots, going clear over Rand's head as he had taken the other by surprise, dropping to the ground, had caught the other high in the chest, pitching him from the saddle.

'Dead,' said Merriam. The banker had stepped forward, bent over the other. 'Must've been plumb unlucky.' He lifted his head and stared at Rand. 'He had his gun drawn when it happened. Looks to me as if he meant to shoot you in the back.'

Rand gave a quick nod. 'Sure looks that way,' he muttered. 'Guess we'll never know now.' He thrust his gun back into leather, straightened up. He eyed Merriam directly. 'Reckon you won't be needing those Vigilantes of yours now. Those men yonder won't cause you any more trouble.'

'What you intendin' to do now, Kelsey?' asked the other. 'Now that Blane is dead, I reckon we'll be needin' a new lawman around here, a man we can trust and who ain't afraid to face up to a killer.'

'If you're offerin' me the job, I reckon I'll have to turn it down,' Rand said seriously.

'Anythin' to do with what Carver said earlier?' asked the other shrewdly.

Rand pondered that, then shook his head. 'No, nothing to do with that. I suppose he figured he was only doin' what was right, warning me off. But I'm not cut out for a job like this. The war changed a lot of things for a great many men and it brought a kind of restlessness inside me that it's been hard to fight at times. But I know now that if I don't fight it, I'll always have it bucking me.'

'I guess I understand,' nodded the other. 'You'll be riding on west now?'

'That's right,' he nodded. 'It's hell to reach the end of one trail and not know exactly where the next one will start, nor where it will lead you.'

*

Having had one drink in the Golden Belle saloon, Rand moved out of the town, rode slowly along the main street that was no longer a dividing line, but just an ordinary street once again. He paused at the end, turned his head and looked back, fingers hooked beneath the saddle. The dust storm had swept over the place and the sky now had that clear, polished look as if it had been scoured clean by those millions of particles of dust. He sat for a long moment, looking behind him. Then he gigged his mount forward, felt it respond to the slight touch of the spurs. The wooden planks of the bridge creaked a little as he crossed over them, then he was out in the wide valley with the deep, afternoon hush lying all about him. He thought of Jim Turner as he rode, of Colter, Sutton and Tyrone, and quite suddenly, all of those men were a long way from him, their faces had dimmed in his memory and he knew that the hurt that had once been there was fading quickly now. Whether it would leave him completely in time, he did not know. There was the chance that it might if he were able to find something to take its place.

When he got to the top of the long, low rise that lifted clear of the valley at the far end, dipping down on the other side towards the thickly-wooded slopes and the lake which glistened faintly in the early evening sun, he sat quite still in the saddle, rolled himself a smoke and leaned forward, drawing the sweet-smelling smoke deep into his lungs.

For the first time, he knew why he had turned down that offer which Merriam had made to him. He felt the utter peace of this place flood into his mind, relaxing his body, loosening the taut limbs. The horse whickered softly as he reached forward and patted the long neck.

Finishing the smoke, he flicked the stub into the dry earth, watched it glow for a moment before it winked out. Before moving on down the slope he did a strange thing. Reaching inside the jacket, he unpinned the marshal's silver star from his shirt, held it in the palm of his hand for a long moment, staring down at it as if mesmerised. It flashed a little between his fingers and for a brief second they curled tightly about it as if it were something infinitely precious. But it belonged to a time in his life which was past and gone. Lifting his hand, he hurled the badge as far as he could into the tall grass that grew alongside the trail. It flashed once, then vanished from his sight.

Sighing, the breath gusting in his lungs, he rode down the winding trail to where the homestead nestled in the bottom reaches of the valley and as he rode into the courtyard, he saw Lois come out of the doorway and stand on the porch, waiting for him, a smile on her lips.